DEATH OF A
BUSYBODY

DEATH OF A BUSYBODY

GEORGE BELLAIRS

With an Introduction by
MARTIN EDWARDS

This edition published 2016 by
The British Library
96 Euston Road
London
NW1 2DB

Originally published in 1943 by The Macmillan Company

Cataloguing in Publication Data

A catalogue record for this book is available
from the British Library

ISBN 978 0 7123 5644 2

Typeset by Tetragon, London
Printed and bound by
CPI Group (UK) Ltd, Croydon CR0 4YY

CONTENTS

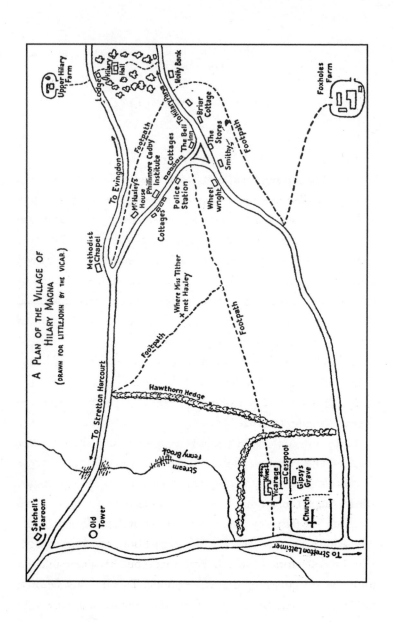

A PLAN OF THE VILLAGE OF HILARY MAGNA
(DRAWN FOR LITTLEJOHN BY THE VICAR)

To Evingdon

Upper Hilary Farm

Lodge

Hilary Hall

Holly Bank

Footpath

Briar Cottage

The Stores

Foxholes Farm

To Hillary Parva

Cadby Cottages

The Bell Inn

Footpath

McHaxley's House

Phillimore Institute

Smithy

Methodist Chapel

Police Station

Wheel wright

Cottages

Where Miss Tither met Haxley

Footpath

Footpath

To Stretton Harcourt

Hawthorn Hedge

Fenny Brook

Stream

Satchell's Tearoom

Old Tower

Well

Cesspool

Vicarage

Gipsy's Grave

Church

To Stretton Latimer

INTRODUCTION

The eponymous nosy parker in *Death of a Busybody* is Miss Ethel Tither. She has made herself deeply unpopular in the quintessentially English village of Hilary Magna, since she goes out of her way to snoop on people, and interfere with their lives. On being introduced to her, the seasoned reader of detective stories will spot a murder victim in the making. Sure enough, by the end of chapter one, this unpleasant lady has met an extremely unpleasant fate. She is found floating in a cesspool, having been bludgeoned prior to drowning in the drainage water.

This is, in every way, a murky business; realizing that they are out of their depth, the local police quickly call in the Yard. Inspector Thomas Littlejohn, George Bellairs' series detective, arrives on the train, and in casting around for suspects, he finds that he is spoiled for choice. The amiable vicar supplies him with a map showing the scene of the crime; maps were a popular feature of traditional whodunnits for many years, and Bellairs occasionally included them in his books, as he does here.

Death of a Busybody was Bellairs' third novel, published in 1942. First editions in dust jackets of his early books are much sought after by collectors, and fetch high prices, but Bellairs' name has long been forgotten by the wider public. This is a pity, because he wrote amusing stories that afforded his readers welcome light relief during the grim war years, and then in the decades that followed. His work was not dazzlingly original – the plot device that supplies a crucial alibi in this story, for instance, is a variation on a theme that had become very familiar to crime fans by the time the book was published – but his humour means that his books do not plod dully, like so many worthy police stories of the time. There is another feature of Bellairs' writing that appealed to his original readers, and remains attractive today. Time and again in his work, he makes clear that he detests sanctimony, hypocrisy, and greed, although he makes his points with a light touch. One suspects that, during his day job as a bank manager, he came across a good deal of the worst of human nature, and found in writing detective fiction a pleasing form of catharsis.

George Bellairs was a pseudonym masking the identity of Harold Blundell (1902–1982), one of the few bankers to write crime fiction, rather than feature in it as a murder victim or rascally suspect. Blundell started work at the age of fifteen with the Lancashire and Yorkshire Bank, which merged with Martin's Bank in 1928; he remained with Martin's until his retirement in 1962. In 1941, he published his first novel, *Littlejohn on Leave*, a book which is now a great rarity. He said that he chose a pen-name to fit with the initials of his wife, Gwladys Blundell. The late R.F. Stewart, who wrote a fascinating article about Bellairs for the crime fanzine *CADS* in 1994, hypothesized that the chosen forename represented a tribute to Georges Simenon, creator of Maigret, who was an influence on Bellairs' crime writing.

At the time when he wrote this book, Blundell was working in a bank by day, and also acting as an air raid warden, being exempt from military service because he was blind in one eye; he found that writing a detective story helped to pass the time during the blackout. His debut novel introduced Inspector Thomas Littlejohn of Scotland Yard, who became his regular series character, appearing in all but one of the fifty-eight Bellairs novels (the exception, a 1943 book called *Turmoil in Zion*, featured Inspector Nankivell, a not dissimilar character). Blundell also published four crime novels between 1947 and 1950 under the guise of Hilary Landon.

The George Bellairs books were published in the United States, and translated into French and other languages, but writing was first and foremost a hobby for Blundell, who became a popular public speaker; he once said that nobody wanted to hear him talk about banking once they discovered that he wrote detective stories. Because he was so prolific, the quality of his work was variable, but his best novels supply pleasant entertainment.

Blundell gained a staunch supporter in Francis Iles (also known to detective fiction fans as Anthony Berkeley), who had mysteriously abandoned a successful career as a crime writer, and become a highly regarded reviewer. Iles was good at spotting crime-writing talent – he was one of the first critics to identify the potential of P.D. James and Ruth Rendell – and he regarded Bellairs as under-rated. The two men became friendly, and Iles encouraged Blundell to negotiate improved terms with his publisher (whose contract Iles, never a man to sit on the fence, described as "utterly iniquitous… the worst I've ever seen"). Blundell, however, seems not to have been a man to drive a hard bargain.

Because he did not depend on writing as his main source of income, he was able to write for pleasure rather than profit, and he continued to produce stories about Littlejohn for those same publishers until the end of his life. Such an unassuming fellow would no doubt have been startled, as well as gratified, to learn that his work is now reaching new readers in the twenty-first century as part of the series of Crime Classics published by the British Library. Yet it is a just reward for a likeable author who, as R.F. Stewart said, "gave pleasure to thousands of readers and retained a faithful following over forty years... For a bank manager that is not a bad epitaph".

MARTIN EDWARDS
www.martinedwardsbooks.com

CHAPTER I

The Body by the Gipsy's Grave

THE SEPTEMBER MORNING WHICH GREETED THE REV. Ethelred Claplady, M.A. (Cantab.), incumbent of Hilary Magna (and Parva for that matter), made him want to leap and shout. "He slept till break of day and then he awoke and sang", lisped the vicar to himself, flinging wide the casement, stretching out his thin, pyjama-clad arms as if embracing the whole scene, and standing on his bony tiptoes in a posture which suggested that he was about to launch himself into space. Then, expanding his narrow chest, he took a deep and noisy breath. The sudden inrush of tonic air made him light-headed and he reeled back a pace, clutching wildly at the edge of his dressing-table for support. Gingerly, he clawed his way back to the bed where, having rested himself, he disentangled his heavy, camel-hair dressing-gown from a confusion of blankets and sheets and, swathing his shivering body in it, mentally cautioned himself against overdoing his breathing exercises. Better go gently, one nostril at a time, as in Yoga. Feeling better, he pattered to the bathroom on the other side of the house. There, he tripped to the window again, closed his eyes and one side of his nose and gently inhaled to the accompaniment of uplifting thoughts. The result was remarkable, for on this wing of the vicarage the air was no longer champagne, but a veritable blast from Gehenna filled with death and corruption. Mr. Claplady's eyes opened and closed rapidly and wildly, he snuffled like a dog exploring his favourite tree and hastily deflated his lungs, wrestling inwardly to eject the last cubic centimetre of the foulness he had drawn in, and then rushed back to the fresher side of the building.

All around nature spread her rich cloak of autumn colour. Viewed from the vicar's bedroom, the trees of his garden and the adjacent churchyard framed a magnificent view of the flat fields surrounding the ancient church with its square tower and crooked weathercock; the trim lawns round the old house; cattle standing mutely chewing in the field beyond the hedge; a few rabbits sporting among the laden apple trees in the orchard; and the gardener with his head among the tops of the potatoes which he was disinterring, his huge backside protruding like some monstrous, black toadstool. Widespread fields of corn, ripe and ready for harvest. The whole scene gently softened by a thin mist although the morning was well advanced. The vicar sighed. On this, of all mornings, old Gormley, the general handyman of the village, had decided to empty the clerical cesspool. "And man alone is vile…" mused the Reverend Claplady to his image in the mirror as he shaved in the room to leeward. He hurried, as it was past ten o'clock. He had overslept through late work the night before.

The face which confronted him in the looking-glass was a puzzle to its owner. Day after day, for fifty-two years, the Rev. Ethelred had seen it over and over again as he contorted it and slowly scraped the lather from it, yet he had no idea what it looked like to others. His photographs, taken at parish garden parties, rummages, cricket matches, floral fêtes, when he held the seat of honour in the centre of the front row of his self-conscious looking flock, and the more formal portraits executed for the local press when he became incumbent of the Hilarys, to say nothing of that for his passport (in which he resembled a bogus clergyman fleeing from justice), always came as a shock to him. Somehow, he knew every feature; high, wide forehead with dark, thin hair brushed tightly back, brown eyes, rather close-set in deep sockets beneath bushy black brows, a thin face with a waxy skin and a bony, projecting chin, blue from a quick-growing beard and careless shaving. The mouth was large and generous and the nose straight and regular, a perfect figure 4 in symmetry and style, with wide nostrils and a pink-shot-purple hue, suggestive of indigestion. Funnily enough, Ethelred Claplady could have enumerated every detail of his face and even assembled them all like a strange jigsaw into something like order, but the resulting picture conveyed nothing to him. Every morning, as he confronted his reflection through a froth of shaving-soap, he puzzled over it. The good man's musings on his own baffling image were interrupted by the sight of two familiar figures engaged in conversation in the field-path which skirted his garden. He could well imagine what was going on. It was Miss Tither, the village busybody, continuing her ceaseless campaign to convert Mr. Haxley, the local atheist, to the orthodox faith.

Miss Tither, "rather long in the tooth", as the Squire described her, was about fifty years of age and had sufficient means to pay for the domestic help which released her to poke her nose into the affairs of everyone for miles around. She was scorned and snubbed by most, but carried on her secret investigations and remedial campaigns against vice and sin with abhorrent fortitude. The village quailed in fear of her. Husbands, raising their hands or voices against their wives, paused at the thought of her. Scolding wives pitched their nagging in a lower key, lest Miss Tither should be in the offing. The lecherous, adulterous, drunken and blasphemous elements of the population held her in greater fear than the parson and looked carefully over their shoulders lest she be in their tracks. Lovers in the Hilarys never embraced or kissed in fields or coppices under the open sky, but sought the dark depths of woods and spinneys for their ecstasies, lest the all-seeing Titherian eye light on them from the blue or through rifts in the clouds. The ungodly, unpatriotic, radical and dissenting sections of the community gave her a wide berth, for she clung like a leech when she buttonholed them, wasted their time, reviled the views they held dear, and made them wish to strike her dead. Her battle against what she deemed to be sin and shame, however, did not end in ferreting out offences. Had such been the case, she would merely have been regarded as an innocuous busybody, vicariously sinning. Miss Tither was a campaigner as well. Her weapon was her tongue, which she used like a pair of bellows, fanning a spark of a whisper into a consuming fire of chatter, a holocaust of pursuing flame.

From his place at his bedroom window, the vicar could only dimly recognize the distant figures, but his imagination filled in the details, especially those of Miss Tither. She wore a knitted costume which seemed to have expanded in the wash and hung on her bony, tall frame like a sack. The long, shapeless skirt drooped round her thin, grey-stockinged ankles; the sleeves of the jacket had been turned back to give freedom to her ugly wrists and long square hands and fingers, which flapped in energetic gesticulation as she spoke. Grey-streaked dark hair, untidily gathered and tied in a bun perched on the back of the head. From the mass of hair rose a black straw hat, a cross-breed between a bonnet and a straw beehive. A long, narrow face, with a good pink skin; firm, rounded chin; large mouth, with fleshy lips, the nether one projecting aggressively. Large, slightly protruding, cunning, grey eyes, set in dark circles under thin black brows and a broad, low forehead. The nose, however, was the dominating feature of the face. Long, fleshy and slightly tilted at the tip, with narrow nostrils. A sensitive, inquisitive organ, built for foraging and rooting, and always in a condition, judging from its colour and sniffing, of impending cold in the head.

Mr. Haxley, her victim, stood good-naturedly listening to her arguments. A stocky, rotund man, with a square face framed in a short, curly brown beard and with sparkling, grey eyes behind gold-rimmed, bifocal glasses. He was a man of means, although nobody quite knew where his money came from. There were dark surmises, of course, ranging from activities on the turf to dirty work in Buenos Aires, but the truth was that he had successively married and survived three ladies of property and lived on their accumulated fortunes. He rented fifty acres of glebe from Mr. Claplady for shooting purposes (it was good for little else), and twice a week could be seen prowling round with his gun and blazing away at sitting rabbits and perching wood-pigeons, greatly to the disgust of the local gentry, who dubbed him an unsportin' bounder and passed him by with throaty noises and popping, bile-shot eyes. Mr. Haxley contended that killing outright a stationary quarry was more humane than scaring it into activity and then sending it squealing to cover with a shattered wing or a peppered rump. He was a well-read man, especially in theology. He never attended church, but relished an argument with the vicar, whose knowledge of and beliefs in the Thirty-Nine Articles of Religion he loved to prove and find wanting. Miss Tither frequently assailed him with tracts and pamphlets which called on him to Turn or Burn, Repent and Be Saved, Beware of the Wrath to Come, and Prepare to Meet Thy God. As the vicar watched them, Miss Tither took from her bag a fistful of papers, waved them excitedly and pressed them between Mr. Haxley's well-kept hand and the gun he was holding and he accepted the gift with a smile and a courteous bow. The vicar descended to breakfast.

Having attended to his morning mail and pushed aside three bills, four begging letters, an advertisement for unbreakable celluloid clerical collars and a booklet on glandular therapy, the reverend gentleman rose, wiped the grease from his chin and the marmalade from his lips and set forth on his daily round.

He found Gormley shovelling metallic-looking slime from the cesspool into a wheelbarrow. The Parsonage Hinnom was in a ditch at the bottom of the orchard hidden by a screen of lush nettles and towering golden-rod, nurtured to gigantic propor-tions by the fertilizing refuse. The labourer raised a crafty face, sunbaked and framed in a fringe of shaggy whiskers. His small, cunning eyes shone venomously.

"That fellow did say you could drink the water if so minded," he exclaimed to himself and spat in the drainage in which he paddled with no concern. This was a recurrent thrust, aimed by Gormley at the vicar every time the job was done. The glib-tongued cesspool salesman who sold Mr. Claplady the outfit had sworn that it would totally consume any solid or liquid meal imposed on it, leaving, as the only by-product, a stream of pure water and the good man had taken him at his word, in spite of the doubts expressed in very forthright language by Isaiah Gormley. This ignoring of his counsel, which was paramount to all in his teeming family circle except his principal daughter-in-law, added to the failure of the scheme which necessitated Gormley's descending into the miniature Tophet to clear it every six months, was a standing grievance. The vicar was, on this morning, however, in no mood to bandy words.

"Get on with your work, Isaiah. Every time a sheep baahs, it loses a bite, you know," he said, and then more sternly, "I wish too, that you'd see that the wind is blowing *away* from the vicarage when you decide to clear out this place. Most unhealthy and unpleasant with the wind in the south-west. Most unpleasant."

"There's nuttin' healthier for man or beast," came the voice of the aged one from below ground, and his voice, echoed by the metal tank, took on the brassy resonance of some hidden oracle. "Makes things thrive and grow," boomed out from the earth, as though the cesspool itself were trumpeting its claim to virtue.

"Don't talk nonsense, Gormley, and get on with it," said Mr. Claplady and passed on.

There was a scuffling in the ditch and the angry face and then the indignant body of Isaiah emerged. No furriner was going to tell him what was right or wrong about prevailing winds and odours in his native village, not even the vicar. In dudgeon, he covered up the sewage-hole with its metal plates, stamped angrily on them, left the job half finished and stumped off in the direction of the village pub. He was going on strike!

Mr. Claplady, unaware of Gormley's defection, passed on to his pastoral duties. He had a call to make at the church and then sick visiting to attend to. He was ruffled at Gormley's impudence and to clear his mind, adopted a mental device which he erroneously thought he had invented himself, of concentrating on and reciting aloud the first piece of poetry that came into his mind.

> I remember, I remember
> The house where I was born...

muttered Mr. Claplady as he moved to the centre of the village of Hilary Magna.

Sick missioning did not take Mr. Claplady long that day. His principal client was Mr. Allnutt, grocer and vicar's warden, now laid low with lumbago. The shopkeeper was cantankerous and gave his father-confessor short shrift, for he was champing at the bit in his bedroom over the shop, listening to the ceaseless tinkle of the bell over the door below, wondering whether his assistant was relaxing in matters of weights and measures and slacking or indulging in dalliance with the girls of the village. Mr. Claplady made a speedy exit, overcome by the reek of liniment and rubbing-bottles.

In the High Street, the parson encountered the daughter-in-law of Isaiah Gormley, a lazy, prolific woman, five of whose six children had been removed to the isolation hospital, suffering from the prevailing epidemic of scarlet fever. She was standing in the doorway of a small cottage, suckling her latest arrival from a copious breast. She wore a glazed, ecstatic look, her hair was unkempt, her face dirty and her house filthy. *Lutulentus sus* came wilfully into the good man's mind as he remembered the reference being made to his own untidy desk and copy-books by his latin master in student days.

Mrs. Gormley, junior, was chattering.

"It's an ill wind, I allus sez," she clattered on, half choking her infant by pressing the flowing fount over its face. "A perfect 'oliday fer me, it is. I doan't know I'm alive with the five of them away... not that I doan't miss 'em. But I 'ope they doan't come back too quick. An 'oliday it is for them, too."

Mr. Claplady retreated feeling depressed. All his efforts to improve conditions of life and thought in the village by lectures, literature and sermons, seemed to fall on stony ground. But he must not despair. No, he must cast despond from his mind. Again, he applied his little remedy of reciting to himself the first line of poetry that entered his head.

> They say the Lion and the Lizard keep
> The Courts where Jamshid gloried and drank deep,
> And Bahram, the great Hunter, the wild Ass
> Stamps o'er his Head, but cannot break his Sleep.

Suddenly realizing with horror, this scrap of infidelity flung up by his mind, the vicar turned his thoughts elsewhere, to Gormley, whom he thought still engaged in his noisome labours.

Isaiah was not far away. As the parson left the cottage of his son, his dirty, bearded face appeared round the side of the house. His daughter-in-law's complacency left her.

"Wot you doin' 'ere this time o' day?" she yelled. "Ain't you got a full day's work along o' the vicar's drain...?"

Old Gormley quailed. He was afraid of his son's wife.

"I bin an' gone on strike, I 'ave. Nobody, not even parson, be goin' to critikize the work I be doin'. I give it up and left 'un to do it 'isself."

He bared his toothless gums at this idea of a joke. Mrs. Gormley, junior, shrieked, but not with mirth. The smell of ale was on the air around the old curmudgeon, too.

"Strike, did yer say, yer hidle, lazy, boozy old gufernuttin. As if I 'adn't enough mouths to feed on Joe's wage, without you spongin' on me fer meat and drink. Get you back to work an' quick about it, an' doan't you go playin' and gossupping on the way. Either you pays me the five bob vicar promised when you comes by it to-night, or else you finds bed and board elsewhere. No room fer scroungin' old dodgers at this 'ouse. So be off with yer..."

Before the tirade subsided, Gormley was off across the field to the vicarage again. Anywhere for refuge from the searing tongue. The squealing of his barrowwheel died away in the distance. Gormley had another reason for hurrying. Ahead of him he recognized the figure of the vicar, making for the short cut to his house through the churchyard, over the wall of which lay the cesspool. He must have the lid off and be making a show of working before Mr. Claplady reached him. Otherwise, he might get the sack and then, no five shillings and... He broke into a shambling trot, his barrow leaping over stones in the field-path.

Meanwhile, the vicar, meditating and serene again, had reached God's acre and was almost within the range of the savoury smell of the roast beef, Yorkshire pudding and apple-dumplings cooking for his lunch, when a thought struck him. In unconsecrated ground by the churchyard hedge, overlooking the terminus of the vicarage drainage-system, stood a gipsy's grave, marked by a large stone erected by the Romanies in honour of their lost queen. Prior to Mr. Claplady's arrival in Hilary, it bore, unchallenged, a strange inscription.

> Darker and darker the black shadows fall.
> Death and oblivion reign over all.

On entering his new field of labour, the good man had been shocked at the dark, hopeless sentiments allowed to exist in the memorial rhyme. He made up his mind to remedy the evil at once, but pressure of other things had deferred it. Last week, however, he had, at his own expense, instructed the stone mason to carve a remedial line on the slab, which now stood out, white and clear, in contrast to the old lettering. "Till the day break and the shadows flee away." The vicar read his handiwork with relish. It lifted his thoughts from the commonplace difficulties of the present and pinned them on the future. His soul seemed to take wings and soar.

A wild cry brought Mr. Claplady to earth. It was a mixture between the bellow of a bull isolated from his herd, and the groan of a boxer punched in the wind. The vicar peered over the hedge whence the sound had come. Old Gormley stood there, rooted to the spot, beside the tank, the cover of which he had just removed. Perceiving the head of the parson poking over the bushes, he pointed a horny finger at the object he had laid bare. It lay like a sack in the cesspool, face downwards, arms outspread. No need to tell Mr. Claplady what or who it was. The ill-fitting, knitted costume was enough. The vicar uttered a choking scream, which he stifled half-way by putting his hand over his mouth.

"Stay there, touch nothing and let nobody come near," he squealed at Gormley. Then, gathering up his cassock, he ran to the village by the nearest route, stumbling, gasping and clutching his skirts, like an eager entrant in the sack-race at the sports of his Band of Hope.

CHAPTER II

The Policeman's Fun Is Spoiled

P.C. SAM HARRIWINCKLE, REPRESENTATIVE OF LAW AND order in Hilary Magna and Parva, made quite sure that his duties of "keeping an eye on things" took him past the big field of Foxholes Farm when Mr. Wheelwright, the owner, cut the wheat there. It was always a bit of a Derby Day when the event came round. Not only was there a goodly assembly of workers on the job, stooking the sheaves as they were flung from the rattling, thrashing binder and gleaning and tying the loose stuff; there was a shooting-party in attendance as well. The rabbits, hares, wood-pigeons and other brigands of hedge and spinney, which had hitherto enjoyed food and lodging among the golden crop, bolted for cover as activities in the surrounding corn alarmed them. Four local gentlemen of leisure arrived with their guns at the invitation of the farmer and, stationed one at each corner of the diminishing rectangle of wheat, blazed away at the flee-ing vermin. They brought lunch baskets, too, and bottled beers, which they immersed in the cool water of a spring under one of the hedges until required. P.C. Harriwinckle was partial to veal-and-ham pie, cold chicken and good ale and the sportsmen, flushed with the forenoon's victories over fur and feather, were generous in sharing at mealtime.

As the constable crossed the fields leading from his cottage to Foxholes Farm, the banging of guns and the clatter of machinery announced that operations had begun. Sam walked sedately, as though conducting an ordinary routine patrol, but he was all agog to be reaching his destination. He drew out a watch like a turnip and gravely consulted it.

"H'm," he said to himself. "Nice time. Ha' past eleven. Knock-off for dinner at twelve-thirty or thereabouts. Mustn't look as if I'd come cadgin'. Gimme time to walk around, be a bit sociable-like, and then be inwited to a bite o' lunch."

And he nodded to himself at the cunning of his strategy and passed a red handkerchief across his mouth, which was moist from thoughts of the good things to come.

"I thought we'd be seeing the bobby about feeding time," said Mr. Wheelwright, chuckling and pointing to a helmet bobbing over the hedge, as the constable made his way to the gate of the cornfield.

"Mornin', Mr. Wheelwright," said Harriwinckle, sidling up and surveying the scene with a businesslike air, as if making sure that all present were honest and of good report. "You got a good day for your cuttin' agen, and a rare crop you 'ave, to be sure. Thought I'd just call as I was passin' this way and see how you was getting along. Makin' good progress, eh?"

"Yes. Everything going fine and the girls taking the places of the men splendidly," replied the farmer, indicating three land-girls briskly at work. The sturdy shire horses clopped round and round the field, shying now and then as a stray No. 5 from one of the guns flew past ears or flanks. "Fine-bone! Captain!" yelled the girl on the seat of the binder, calling them to order.

"Still stick to yer hosses, Mr. Wheelwright," commented the policeman. "Now, wot I do like to see, is a good hoss. Better'n any tractor, to my mind, though not as fast, not as fast, you'll 'ave to admit."

"No, Sam, but I can't bring my mind to sellin' that pair. When they're past working, I guess I'll not replace them. I use the tractor for ploughing and the like, but I do like to see a good team afore the binder. Old fashioned, I am. Well, I must be seein' to things."

P.C. Harriwinckle began a round of formal visits to various parts of the field. He visited the men with guns, counted their victims, praised their aim and admired their dogs. They, with one eye on the field, returned his cheerful wishes and Stevenson, the best shot and most genial of the quartette, invited him to help himself to a drink, when so disposed.

"Thankee, Mr. Stevenson," said the bobby. "I'll just wait till the binder stops. I like to watch the sport and wouldn't miss it." Which was as good as inviting himself to lunch. Stevenson, with a twinkle in his eye, suggested that a bit of pie might go well with the ale later and Harriwinckle's heart grew glad under his tunic. Just then, Coleman's gun banged, first one barrel and then the other. He was the poorest shot of the party and his quarry still survived, struggling, limping to the hedge. Either someone would have to make a run for it, or the poor, maimed thing would get away. P.C. Harriwinckle rose to the occasion. He was a heavy, florid man, but he could pick up his feet when the occasion demanded it. He set off like a charging bull after the rabbit, overtook it, drew his truncheon and finished it off. Work and shooting hung fire and the rest of the party watched the policeman's progress with growing hilarity. There was a faint cheer and much laughter as he captured his prize. Mr. Wheelwright, who had first claim to the day's bag, made no bones about giving the spoils to the winner.

"It's all yours, Sam," he said to the sweating policeman, who now stood rather shamefacedly mopping his brow, neck and ears with his red handkerchief. Sam was feeling that, somehow, he had upset his dignity by his impulsive chase, but the goodwill of the spectators reassured him. Someone mentioned lunch and he quite recovered his poise. Stevenson sent one of the girls to fish out the beers from their cool cache, and lunch boxes and baskets were brought out. But poor P.C. Harriwinckle was doomed to have his fun spoiled.

"Isn't that your youngest running across the path there?" said Mr. Wheelwright, pointing to a small, sturdy figure, panting excitedly over the meadow adjacent to the cornfield.

"Yes. That's 'arry," replied his father. "I wonder what he's wantin' at this hour. Sometin' must 'ave 'appened."

Young Harry entered the field, brandishing a paper and gesturing to his father, who strode to meet him.

"Wot you wantin', Harry?" asked his parent sternly, still red and puffing from his own exertions. The boy was too breathless to answer and pushed his message into his father's hand. The constable read it and whistled.

"'Ere," he added to his youngest, handing him the rabbit to which he still clung. "'Ere, take that straight home to your mother an' no playin' on the way. Now run along, like a good lad. Do you know wot's in this note?"

"Yes, dad. I saw Mr. Claplady write it in our house. Old Tither's dead, ain't she?"

"Old 'oo?"

"Miss Tither, dad."

"That's better and don't let me 'ear you say anythin' so disrespec'ful of the dead agen. And, mind you, not a word about this to anybody."

"It's all over the village already, dad."

Which was true. Mr. Claplady, assisted by adrenalin poured into his blood-stream by his excited glands, had bounded over fields and ditches straight to the policeman's cottage, followed by the eyes of a score or more villagers, whom he passed on the way. Mrs. Harriwinckle, a buxom, busy, broad-beamed woman, was draping the washing over the bushes in the garden when the parson arrived and for a minute after hearing the news stood petrified, holding her husband's nightshirt like one wrestling with a ghost. Mr. Claplady hung suspended over the garden gate, recovering his breath whilst she informed him that her husband was not in.

"He's probably at Wheelwright's big field along o' Foxholes Farm. They'm cutting there to-day and he never misses that or the lunch that goes with it. He did say he wouldn't be 'ome to his dinner, so like as not you'll find him there."

"Oh dear, oh dear," gasped the vicar. "I'm all in and don't feel capable of hurrying another yard, Mrs. Harriwinckle."

Just then, young Harry hove in sight, coming from school, but manifested a disposition to take the path to the nutbushes rather than the way home. His mother spotted him.

"Harreeeeee!" she shrieked. "Come you 'ere at once."

Young Harry Harriwinckle showed a tendency to deafness.

"Harreee… come 'ere this minute, or I'll tan the hide off yer," yelled his mother. Whereat, the youngster made for home with leaden steps.

"Perhaps he'd better take a note," said Mr. Claplady, as the
constable's youngest gave him a baleful, disrespectful glance. "May
I write somewhere?" Mrs. Harriwinckle showed the parson into
the front room, where stood her husband's desk and other official paraphernalia. She produced a sheet of notepaper, an almost
empty bottle of thick ink and a scratchy pen, and passed her apron
over a chair, removing all the dust that wasn't there in a homely
gesture. Mr. Claplady wrote with difficulty and in a jerky hand.

My dear Harriwinckle,
    Come at once. Miss Tither found dead in vicarage ditch.
Fear violence. ETHELRED CLAPLADY, Vicar.

He folded the note and handed it to Harry, with a penny. The
lad regarded the solitary coin in his palm without enthusiasm,
whereat the vicar added another to it.

"Now jest you be off, 'arry, and don't play on the way. Else
I'll tell yer father to tan yer when he comes in," threatened his
mother. The threat seemed effective and Harry cantered off,
immersed in thoughts of how to get the most for his twopence,
rather than those of violence, in the village. But others were
deeply concerned.

Old Andrew Pepperdy happened to be hedging just by the
garden of the police station and overheard the vicar's tale. He
tottered off to the Bell Inn as fast as his old legs would bear him,
for a pint and the glory of being first with the news.

"Old Ethel Tither's been murdered in vicar's garden," said he
gasping from his efforts, "vicar's just bin to p'lice station with the
news. All of a tucker he be. Gimmeapint."

The baker's boy from Evingdon, the nearest town, four miles away, happened to be at "The Bell" delivering bread at the time and, bounding into his van, tore along the road, hurling out loaves and the scandal to his customers.

"Ethel Tither's bin found strangled in the vicarage."

"Miss Tither's bin found shot in vicar's orchard."

"Owld Tither's bin done-in. They say the vicar's done it."

These and the like flew round the countryside like news from African jungle-drums. Women ran from house to house and from cottage to cottage. Telephones were busy among the better classes. Roadmen yelled it at passers-by. Schoolchildren took it home on their ways from school. The postman made a special round for the joy of sensationmongering. When P.C. Harriwinckle arrived at his house, he was surrounded by a curious crowd. Where? How? When? Who? They riddled him with queries and he, good man, now calm and bearing his responsibilities with portentous dignity, gave the same answer to each. "I am, as yet, in no position to make a public statement. Matters is well in 'and and I'll trouble you all to go calmly to your 'omes and about your businesses, else I'll 'ave to take a few names for h'obstruction and causing commotion."

The crowd regarded him with awe. He seemed to have grown in stature and importance. The guardian angel, the protector of them all against a similar fate to Miss Tither's, the avenging hound who would see justice done. Only Old Pepperdy, fortified by his pint and disgusted because he'd had to pay for it himself, dared raise his voice.

"Yah," he said and spat in the road. "Yah! This bain't a job fer a village bobby. This be a Scockland Yard job, this be. You and the locals won't solve him in a month o' Sundays."

"I'll trouble you to be off, Andy Pepperdy, and keep a respec'ful tongue in yer 'ead. Ditchin's your job, so be about it. Hoff you go, afore I takes yer name."

"Takes me name, indeed... bah..." snarled the ancient and was led off protesting by his son-in-law, who feared the old chap might become a suspect himself unless he were silenced. The constable hurried indoors, bustled to the telephone and rang up Dr. Codrington of Evingdon and the Police Inspector there. Then, he careered off to the vicarage to investigate the case.

P.C. Harriwinckle was annoyed to find Isaiah Gormley in charge at the scene of the crime. Unable to control the motley crowd of curious onlookers, which had assembled as soon as the news circulated in the village, the old man had sent for reinforcements in the shape of two of his sons, John Henry and George Hackingsmith, the latter called after a wrestler much admired by his sire in early days, but whose name he could not spell. The Gormley trio, all dirty of face, beery in looks and full of importance, were officiously showing-off in their self-appointed vigil. They greeted the policeman like allies. He soon put them in their places.

"Wot are you a-doin' of there, you Gormleys?" said the P.C., elbowing his way through the crowd.

"Keepin' the place undishturbed until the police come," answered the father.

"Well, they are 'ere now and you won't be required no more. All the same, I'm much obliged to yer. Werry sensible of you it wuz, Isaiah."

"Won't it be a pint apiece?"

"No. It will not. I'm surprised at you, thinkin' of rewards and drinkin' at a time like this. Now, you'd better leave us in peace to inwestigate. And you others, be off with the lot of yer. You've jobs to do, 'aven't yer? Get to them, then, or I'll be takin' a few names for impeding an officer in the discharge of his dooties."

The crowd melted and made off to the village emitting a collective rumbling noise of discontent and disappointment.

Dr. Codrington, accompanied by Inspector Oldfield of the Trentshire Constabulary, arrived on the spot a few minutes later. The remains were moved from their odious repository and gently placed on the bank. The doctor, a tall, grey-headed, broad-shouldered physician of the old school, made a nimble examination of the corpse. Oldfield, with the help of an assistant, took photographs of the body as found, and again, after removal from the pit. Mr. Claplady stood by, pale faced and wringing his hands. He kept his eyes on Oldfield, for the thought of the poor remains of his eccentric parishioner made him feel faint. The Inspector was a portly, medium-built man, with a red face, large, useful hands, sleepy, grey eyes and a solemn countenance. He was a native of Yorkshire and very highly thought-of by his superiors. His heavy frame and calm eyes concealed a very lively mind and he was agile in spite of his weight. He shook his head dubiously and wrinkled his nose.

"What a confoundedly awkward place to chuck a body in. It'll have to be sieved, I reckon. Better get some labourer to do it under supervision. Can you suggest anybody, Harriwinckle?"

"There's Gormley, sir. He was cleanin' out the place only this mornin'. In fact, he found the corpse."

"Send for him, then."

Thus was old Isaiah reinstated triumphantly and his renewed labours laid bare Miss Tither's umbrella and handbag.

Meanwhile, the doctor, who had finished his provisional examination, rose from his knees and dried his hands on a bunch of leaves plucked from the hedge.

"She's been dead about two hours, as far as I can see. Probably eleven-thirty or thereabouts. Death might be due to a blow on the back of the head from a blunt instrument, although I suspect, from sounding the chest, that there's water there. In which case, she was only unconscious when thrown in the tank and drowned in about three inches of water. However, the post-mortem'll show. And now I'm off. Can I give you a lift, Inspector?"

"No, thanks, doctor. I'd better stay on a bit and see to things for the inquest. The Chief Constable will want a report, too, and I'll call to see him on the way back."

"All right, Inspector. I'll probably have performed the autopsy by noon to-morrow and I'll advise you right away. See you later." And the doctor drove off.

The remaining party, consisting of the Inspector, the vicar, P.C. Harriwinckle, P.C. Drake of the Evingdon Force, and Gormley, broke up. The parson who, as yet, had taken no lunch, found his appetite unimpaired by the morning's tragedy and invited Inspector Oldfield to take a bite with him. Refreshment was sent out to the constables in the garden and Gormley, who stated that the only sustenance he craved was a pint of ale, had his wish, if not his appetite satisfied.

Inspector Oldfield obtained, over lunch, plenty of background concerning the character, ways of life and peculiarities of the late Miss Tither and spent the rest of the afternoon in attempting to amplify it in the village. He felt that he would have his work cut out to manage the affair, especially as he had others on his hands;

cases of theft from a local munition works, two country house burglaries and a conscientious objector, who had disappeared on being removed from the register and called up for service. He told Sir Francis Winstanley, the Chief Constable, as much when he called to see him at Hilary Hall, between Hilary Magna and Evingdon, later that day.

"I quite agree with you, Oldfield," said Sir Francis, as they discussed the case together over tea, which the considerate Chief had provided. "This murder has come at a most awkward time. Not that you can't handle it, Inspector, but there are limits to what a man can do. Furthermore, there's going to be a lot of work in this case. It's a whole-time job for a first-class man. So far, you say, it might be any one of a score of people this woman seems to have hounded and harried. And those are people whose connections with her are known. How many others are there who feared her without letting a soul know about it and who, driven to desperation, might have finished her when the chance came?"

Oldfield nodded, his mouth full of toast.

"Now, I'm not taking this step without your good will and full concurrence, Inspector," went on Sir Francis, "but I think it will be as well to call in Scotland Yard. You can co-operate with their man, he'll take the burden from your shoulders and, what is most important, you'll have a first-rate colleague with you, instead of a subordinate. What do you say?"

Inspector Oldfield was an ambitious man, but he was eminently reasonable. He had worked with Scotland Yard before and knew that his career would in no way suffer by bringing them in on the case. In fact, it was to his advantage at the present time of pressure to aim at a quick solution of the Hilary crime, and the best means of obtaining this was with the help of the Yard. He, therefore, cordially agreed with his chief.

Later, Sir Francis rang up Scotland Yard and spoke to the Assistant Commissioner, who was an old friend.

"Now look here, Freddie, this is a country case, so don't be sendin' down one of your smart town lads. He'll rub the village the wrong way and shut the locals up like oysters. Let us have a genial, easy-to-get-on-with feller, a countryman himself if possible."

"Don't worry, Frank," came the reply. "I've got the very man for you. He'll be along to-morrow. You'll like him and so will all the villagers, except the one who's done it."

And that is how it was that Inspector Thomas Littlejohn of the C.I.D., caught the noon express from London to Leicester the following day and, changing at the latter place, boarded a slow little train, which, like the rivers of those parts, wandered leisurely into the heart of England. The second journey took so long, with innumerable halts and a jogtrot pace, that the Inspector fell asleep half way. The guard, who seemed to know where each of his customers was bound for, shook him awake at Evingdon.

CHAPTER III

Opening Moves

W HEN THE RAILWAY COMPANY PROPOSED, ALMOST A CEN-
tury ago, to run the line through Evingdon, the local
bigwigs, scared lest smoke-vomiting locomotives should sully
their fair town, raised a storm and mustered influential opposition.
The track was, therefore, made to avoid the place, with the result
that when it dawned on a new generation that a train-stop would
be highly desirable, the railway company, anxious to please, but
unwilling to make a bulge in the permanent way or construct a
branch line, compromised by erecting a station two miles from the
High Street. Littlejohn alighted from the train and found himself in
open country and with nobody there to meet him. The stationmaster hailed the driver and fireman of the engine in friendly fashion,
passed a joke with the guard, intimated that the train might get
under way again, and hurried to collect Littlejohn's ticket.

"Where's the police station here?" asked the detective.

The stationmaster eyed him suspiciously. He wondered if the
train, the company, or himself had committed a penal offence.

"'Ope nothin's wrong, sir," said he.

"No. I'm calling to see my friend Inspector Oldfield, that's all.
What's the quickest way to him?"

The stationmaster pawed his short, white beard.

"Police station's in the High Street and we be two miles from
it 'ere. Ezra Fewkes did bring a passenger for the train in his cab

and if he's not gone back, he'll take you along with him. Short o' that, you'll 'ave to walk, sir."

The old man tottered through the small booking hall and out into the station approach. He blew his whistle feebly, like a football referee who has run twice round the field, and was answered by a jingling of harness and the clop-clop of hooves. Littlejohn, following in the wake of the obliging official, found a four-wheeler of ancient design, driven by an elderly man with a red face and a huge, rambling moustache, drawing up before him. He hesitated. The cab was bright yellow, recently painted, and supported between its shafts the laziest, fattest horse he had ever seen. As though reading his thoughts, the Jehu spoke, his voice gruff and muffled by his whiskers.

"Aw, don't you think you'm arrivin' in the back o' beyond, mister. Petrol shortage have brought the owld cab out agen. Time was when I had a bobbydazzler of a taxi, but as the old cab was good and the old hoss eatin' me out of 'ouse and 'ome on pension like, I sez to myself, Ezra, I sez, 'tis in the national interest fer yew to sell that there taxi, make old hoss work fer 'is keep, and save the petrol fer better things. So 'ere we be…"

"All right, cabby," said Littlejohn, thinking that he could have walked to town and back again during the long rigmarole, "drive me to the police station." And before the man on the box could question him, he plunged into the interior, smelling of straw, new paint and old leather, and was borne off at a dignified pace towards his destination. The Inspector was considering paying-off the slow-moving vehicle and walking the rest of the journey, when it pulled-up of its own accord beside a trim two-seater. The car-driver, who was in police uniform, climbed out and poked his head in the cab.

"Are you Inspector Littlejohn?" he asked.

"I am. Are you Inspector Oldfield?"

"Yes. How are you? I'm sorry I wasn't at the station to meet the tram. The mayor's wife has lost her favourite pomeranian and turned up with a 'calling all cars' demand just as I was setting out to find you. You managed to get a lift, I see." And his eyes twinkled.

"I was bundled into this thing and protests seemed of no avail."

The two men shook hands, the cabby was paid his dues and left behind to pursue his leisurely way home.

Evingdon is a small market town of about 10,000 people and the main road is there called High Street and widens to hold a market-cross which is the bane of motorists, a stately parish church, a street market, held once a week, and a score or more cattle-pens for the weekly cattle-fair. Narrow streets filled with old houses, many of them gracious, picturesque places, over which trippers burst into raptures, straggle from the main thoroughfare. There are a few banks, a hideous multiple store or two, a labour exchange and a modern cinema surrounding the Cross, and between an ivy-covered doctor's house and a horrible chromium and tile "Maison de Coiffure" stands the police station behind a barricade of sandbags. The police car drew up at the door and soon the two Inspectors were sitting smoking in Oldfield's room.

"I don't know whether we ought to have trailed you down here on the Hilary murder case, Littlejohn," said Oldfield, "but our Chief is a hustler and keen on the most up-to-date methods. We've a number of local burglaries and the like on hand and half the men are away on A.R.P. courses and such. This case will probably be a hard nut to crack and I think you'll find it interesting. I'd better just outline it."

He thereupon gave Littlejohn a résumé of the crime, its nature and details of its discovery.

"Hilary Magna is one of two villages—Hilary Parva's the other—which stand side-by-side about four miles from here on the Leicester Road, or rather, just off it. Actually, Hilary Parva's a small offshoot of Magna. About a hundred years ago, the two bachelor brothers at Hilary Hall quarrelled and the younger went off and built himself a place about a mile away. Put up a church, too, and a few houses, just to make a village of his own. The pair of them started a sort of competition as to who could build the most magnificent church, because the one left behind in Magna wasn't going to be outdone and started renovating and adding to his own. The result was they ruined themselves, left two derelict halls and two fine churches, with few to use them and no money to keep 'em up. There's one parson for both now. A decent chap called Claplady. The body of the victim was found at the bottom of his vicarage garden in Hilary Magna."

He produced the photographs he had taken the day before. "Not pleasant to look at, are they? You see, the body was found in the vicar's cesspool. My own view is that somebody thought it a good place for the purpose. It's cleaned out every six months and that happened on the morning of the crime. In the normal course, nobody would open it up again for another half-year; it's the latest type which disposes of its own rubbish and there wouldn't be much left of a body at the end of that time. Unfortunately for whoever planned it, the old chap who was on the job of cleaning out the septic tank left off half-way, went on strike as a protest against something the vicar said to him, closed the thing and adjourned to the local pub. Then, he repented, probably because

he'd not been paid, and returned to his work, only to find he'd
had visitors with something gruesome in his absence."

"But what about the victim, Oldfield? Who is Tither? What
is she?"

"I was coming to that. She's an old maid who lives in Hilary
Magna and about the biggest paul-pry in the county. Nothing
goes on that she doesn't know about, or rather *didn't*. She lived
at Briar Cottage with a maid, who's been with the family since
Ethel and Martha Tither were children. Martha died a couple
of years ago. Now, the peculiar thing about the victim is, that
there was some method behind her peeping and prying. She was
hot on the track of sin with a view of plucking brands from the
burning. Very religious, anxious to save souls from destruction
by converting them from their evil ways. She was a sort of female
Peeping Tom, but when she'd seen what she was after, she didn't
sneak off, satisfied. Oh, no. She was after the culprits with tracts
and entreaties. It didn't do a bit of good, of course. Only made
enemies for her, because she unearthed quite a lot of secrets and
skeletons in closets and people were either afraid of what she
knew, or else hated her for knowing all there was to know about
'em. As far as I can see, there's no hint at blackmail, but if she's
kept filing-cabinets full of her 'cases', she was a dangerous woman
and many's the one who'd probably like to murder her."

Inspector Oldfield opened a drawer of his desk and passed over
a folder of papers on the case.

"There's the police surgeon's report on the P.M. You'll see
that she was hit on the back of the head with a blunt instrument,
might even have been a stone, and then pitched into the cesspit.
But she wasn't quite dead when thrown in and the real cause of

death is drowning. Drowning in four inches of drainage water in which she was found, face down! Can you beat it?"

"What an abominable end, Oldfield."

"Yes. I had a good talk with the vicar yesterday. She was hanging around at the bottom of his orchard about an hour before she was killed, he says. He got up late at ten o'clock or thereabouts, and saw her earnestly conversin' with a chap called Haxley, a retired man who lives at Hilary. The vicar says she was very excited and thrusting papers, apparently tracts, as usual, in his face. We found a bunch of them in her handbag, which was beside the body. 'Prepare to Meet Thy God', they said. Terribly appropriate, don't you think?"

"Was the vicar or Haxley the last man to see her alive?"

"As far as I know, as yet, Haxley was. I haven't been all round the village. Hadn't the time yesterday. I had a talk with the maid, however. Sarah Russell's her name. A pleasant sort of woman, about fifty, same age as the deceased. She came to the family as a young girl from an orphanage and has been there ever since. She said Miss Tither left home about ten and said she'd be in for lunch around twelve-thirty. She didn't know where she was going, although she seems to know all her mistress's business. Miss Tither was a rare one for talking and, living with only one other in the house, she seems to have let off steam to Sarah pretty often."

"What about Miss Tither's money, Oldfield? Has she any relatives and is there a Will?"

"I have an appointment at 4.30, to see Brassey, her lawyer. His place is here on the High Street and you may as well come with me. Then, we'll drive over to Hilary from there and you can get to work on the spot, if you like. I'll be down to see you every day and do what I can, too, but if you take my advice, you'll stay at the inn at Hilary Magna. It's a country pub, but it's in good hands and has modern conveniences, as the adverts say. You'll enjoy it. The 'Unicorn', the only decent place in Evingdon, is a busy place, quite good, but on the main road and it's noisy at night when the transport lorries come rattling through on the way to London. Please yourself, you know, but that's what I'd do."

Littlejohn decided in favour of the Bell Inn at Hilary and Oldfield telephoned there and secured him a room. They went off for their meeting with the lawyer.

Mr. Brassey, of Brassey, Noakes, Hood and Brassey, received them in a large, musty office on the ground floor of an old converted house in the main street. Littlejohn had never met such a funny lawyer. Small, dapper and thin. Brown hair parted in the middle and plastered meticulously to left and to right, giving the whole the impression of being a toupet, instead of natural growth. Face like a house sparrow, perky, alert and on the hunt. Scrupulously correct morning dress, patent leather boots and spats. A large gold watch-chain, supporting a number of seals. Thin, restless hands, with a large ring on the third left finger, as if weightily and securely wedding him to some overpowering woman. Actually, she was small and cowed, but that by the way. Mr. Brassey consulted a ponderous gold hunter, checked it carefully by a long scrutiny of the clock, which, as though to confirm his views, burst into Westminster chimes on the spot. He shook hands with his visitors and waved them to two shiny, mahogany chairs, the seats of which were upholstered in horsehair which Littlejohn felt penetrate his trousers and irritate his skin as he tried to make himself comfortable.

"Now, gentlemen, and what can I do for you?" said Mr. Brassey in a deep bass voice, which astonished Littlejohn for so small a man. Mr. Brassey was very impressive in court.

Oldfield explained the purpose of their visit. The lawyer's face assumed a stern, sour expression.

"Most irregular until after the funeral. I haven't opened the Will yet. It's at the Bank, but I have a copy, as I drew it up for the deceased. I'm anxious to help run down the scoundrel who's done this dirty business, so I'll commit a little breach of routine to show I'm in earnest. But this is in strictest confidence, mark you."

The Inspectors expressed appreciation of his attitude and swore to treat the matter as utterly private.

Mr. Brassey leapt to his feet like a sparrow taking to wing and tugged at a bell-cord by the empty fireplace. Somewhere in the interior of the dark house a bell could be heard jangling. The patter of feet. Enter an elderly lady, proudly and self-consciously supporting the rôle of private secretary to the lawyer.

"Get me Miss Tither's papers, Miss Buckley, if you please."

"Yes, Mr. Brassey." The swift retreat of nervous footsteps along a passage and the speedy return of the spinster and the papers.

Mr. Brassey assumed a pair of heavy, black-rimmed spectacles which almost totally eclipsed his sparrow face, untied the packet, meticulously rolled up the red tape and consulted the documents with a lot of hemming and hawing as he refreshed his memory, which was good and needed no assistance. He carefully tied up the records again, removed his overbearing glasses, cleared his throat and spoke like a judge passing sentence through a megaphone.

"The Will of Miss Tither is a simple one. Let me say, by way of introduction, that the late Joshua Tither, auctioneer of this town, left about £20,000, divided equally between his daughters, whose mother died years before him. His only children, then, were Miss Ethel and Miss Martha. Miss Martha left all she had to her sister, with one exception. There was an annuity of one hundred pounds, payable to Sarah Russell, the maid, on the death of Miss Ethel Tither and if the said Sarah Russell be still in her employ on such event. In other words, gentlemen, Miss Martha was making sure that Russell stayed on with her sister during her lifetime. Miss Martha died two years ago."

The lawyer cleared his throat, closed his eyes as though burrowing deep into his thoughts, opened them suddenly, and resumed.

"Miss Ethel's Will left another annuity of one hundred pounds to Sarah Russell. So, the maid now inherits two hundred a year for life. Then come small legacies of a hundred apiece to the local Cats' Shelter, the Dogs' Refuge, the Irish Donkey Association, the Y.W.C.A. There is a hundred pounds to the manager and staff of the local branch of the Trentshire Bank, too, for their unfailing courtesy—a very pleasant gesture, if I may say so. Next, *Five Thousand Pounds* to the Home Gospel Alliance for Bringing Sinners to Repentance—her favourite charity and, during her lifetime, a cause for which she worked untiringly. The residue to her sole surviving relative, the Rev. Athelstan Wynyard, her cousin germane, who is, I understand, a missionary in the South Seas somewhere. The executors are myself and the Trentshire Bank. I should think Mr. Wynyard will inherit about twenty thousand pounds, as Miss Ethel saved much of her income. That's all, gentlemen."

"Wynyard, eh?" said Oldfield. "He's in England on leave now. Doing a lecture tour, gathering funds for the Mission. He was in Hilary, staying with Miss Tither last week, according to Russell.

He's been advised of the death and will probably have arrived to-day. Well, I'm much obliged for your help, Mr. Brassey. We'll keep our own counsel until the Will's made public."

They bade the lawyer good-day. Leaving the dark office was like emerging from a tunnel into the sunshine.

"And now for Hilary," said Oldfield, as they climbed into the car. "This is going to be interesting. Mr. Wynyard, eh? Well, well. And Sarah Russell might prove a mine of information. She might even have committed the crime herself, although from what I can see of her, she's not that type. Too afraid of vengeance from heaven. She's an Emmanuel's Witness, and for ten years has been courted by the local shepherd of the Flock. Miss Tither didn't approve, however, and said she'd sack her if she talked of getting married. So, to keep her claims to the legacies, poor Sarah had to remain in single blessedness. Now the shepherd can have his one ewe lamb and her two hundred a year in the bargain."

He slipped in the clutch and the car threaded its way through the High Street and into open country on the way to Hilary. As they passed the distant station, a train was just leaving and a thin stream of passengers flowed from the booking-hall. Oldfield caught his breath.

"Talk of the devil. There's Wynyard! Must have come by that train."

A tall, portly, pompous-looking man, clad in black and wearing a broad-brimmed, black felt hat, was emerging and bearing a bulky gladstone-bag.

"Looks as if he's come to stay for some time," muttered Oldfield.

"You don't seem to like Wynyard, Oldfield."

"You've said it, Littlejohn. He lectured in Evingdon while he was stopping with Miss Tither. Talked about the South Seas at the parish church men's club. The rector persuaded me to go. I'm a Baptist, but I'm not bigoted and I like the rector, so I turned up. I never heard such a lot of sentimental tosh. The man talks like the god and king of the Islands of the Sea, as he calls 'em. Bombastic, conceited bloke if you ask me."

"Going to give him a lift to Hilary?" chuckled Littlejohn.

"No fear! Let him have a ride in Ezra Fewkes's cab. I don't wish him any harm, but I hope the cab's booked-up and he has to walk. Take some of the fat from him. There's a 'bus in another hour's time. He can wait for that."

Oldfield accelerated gleefully, leaving the missionary behind vainly peering for a conveyance.

CHAPTER IV

The Vessel of Wrath

T HE DETECTIVES' FIRST PORT OF CALL WAS THE VICARAGE at Hilary Magna, where the Rev. Ethelred Claplady received them cordially. He was more than pleased to hear that Littlejohn proposed to take up his quarters in the village. The big, comfortable Scotland Yard man inspired confidence and calmed the vicar's spirit, for the thought of harbouring a murderer in his little community appalled him. He even offered Littlejohn a room in his home.

"No thanks, sir," replied the Inspector. "If the Bell Inn is like other country pubs I know, it is the centre of gossip and a good place for overhearing the exchange of news and views. I can spend some profitable nights in the parlour there, I think."

"Oh, you're sure to do that, Inspector. The people in these parts are hospitable and talkative enough and soon grow accustomed to strangers. If I may say so, you're the type which will mix well with them and, after a night there, all reserve will be broken. They'll talk before you and even *to* you as if you were a native."

Oldfield interposed. "We'd better be getting to the scene of the crime before the dusk falls. Perhaps you'd care to join us, vicar? We can talk on the way."

The vicar hastened to find his hat and gloves. The detectives heard him calling to them from upstairs.

"If you like to come upstairs to my room, I'll show you the last place at which I saw poor Miss Tither alive."

They mounted the dark, old stairs and joined the vicar. He pointed to a gap in the hedge beyond the orchard. The manœuvre did not do much good, but it seemed to please the good man. He radiated helpfulness. Littlejohn felt a bit sorry for him. His clothes were neat but threadbare, he looked thin and lonely, and the presence of visitors seemed to overjoy him. Evidently having a struggle with a poor living, apathetic parishioners and lack of sympathy.

"Was Miss Tither still talking to Haxley when you left the window?" queried Oldfield.

"Yes. He must have been the last to see her alive, I should think,... except the murderer. Oh dear."

They descended and crossed the back lawn to the ditch below the churchyard. The cesspit, with its closed iron lid, was shown to Littlejohn. The vicar pointed out the gipsy's grave which he had been contemplating when Gormley found the body.

Littlejohn turned to Oldfield.

"Were there any strange footprints or other signs of whoever carried the body here?"

"No. First, Old Gormley stumped up and down the place, then a crowd gathered from far and wide. By the time Harriwinckle, the policeman, arrived, it was trampled about as if there'd been a cattle fair here. You'll observe, however, that the trees overhanging this ditch make an excellent screen. She could have been struck down several fields away and dragged or carried under cover without anyone seeing, from a distance, what was going on. I tackled Haxley about her early morning assault on him. He said he met her crossing the field towards the main road as though bent on some earnest errand, and she took the opportunity of handing him a tract and calling upon him to repent his doubting ways and see the Light. She left him, apparently, a few minutes after the vicar saw them, and Haxley went on with his shooting."

"Yes, I heard his gun go off a time or two as I went on my way," interposed the clergyman.

"That is so. Southwell the farmer met Haxley about eleven in his fields more than a mile from the vicarage. They stayed talking for about an hour, arranging for some new shooting for Haxley. I've had a word with Southwell; Haxley mentioned their meeting, so I thought I'd confirm it and give him a rough alibi."

"Did anyone else see Miss Tither after Haxley left her, Oldfield?"

"So far, I haven't been able to find out. Perhaps you'll have more luck."

Littlejohn turned to the vicar, who seemed to feel himself somewhat of an intruder in the investigation and was nervously prodding the turf with the toe of his shoe.

"The main point to begin with, Mr. Claplady, is to find out who wanted to stop Miss Tither's mouth, to put it vulgarly. I gather she was invariably hot on the trail of the black sheep of the village."

The vicar showed great eagerness to be of service.

"Oh yes. She unearthed some pretty scandals in her time, you know. She frequently buttonholed me in the vestry and unburdened her mind to me. She pretended to ask my advice, too, but I think that was merely an excuse to tell me what she was going to do. Her mind was usually made up beforehand. A strong-minded, determined woman where sin was concerned."

"What kind of sin?"

"Well—ahem—I'm afraid it was mainly sexual, although there were other things of course."

"Such as…?"

"Mr. Haxley, for example. He's a confirmed agnostic. Perhaps you'll think that doesn't reflect much credit on me. But I've tried, oh dear, I've tried to persuade him that his attitude is foolish. No Creator in the Universe, and such beliefs! Mr. Haxley is a clever man, however, and able to give a Roland for any Oliver in argument. We agreed to differ and be friends, long ago. Miss Tither, though, wouldn't give up. She pursued him relentlessly. I think he derived a lot of good-natured amusement from her sallies, but certainly not a desire to kill her."

"Anything else?"

"Most of the villagers are nominally orthodox and belong to my church. There's a sprinkling of Methodists. They worship in the corrugated iron structure between the two villages. Also, about ten or a dozen Emmanuel's Witnesses, converted from the other faiths by the local leader, Mr. Walter Thornbush, who is also village wheelwright, worship at his cottage. Miss Tither didn't seem to mind what faith people embraced, provided it was Christian and they behaved themselves."

"Let me see, is this Thornbush the man who's courting Miss Tither's servant?"

"That's the man." The vicar smirked and lowered his voice almost to a whisper. "A very worthy man, very worthy and well meaning, but with little religious stock-in-trade other than a profound knowledge of the Psalms. In fact, his conversation when not in the form of sermons, is… is one long Psalmody. You'll be meeting him, I think. He has almost taken up his residence at the Tither home. Comforting and directing the maid, whom he will now be able to marry, after years of waiting. You see, Miss Tither opposed the marriage for some reason and Sarah, the maid, ran the risk of losing quite a considerable annuity under Miss Martha Tither's will if she left Miss Ethel's service."

"Forgive me pressing the sins, sir, but what else did the deceased specialize in in that line?"

"Drink. Domestic turmoil. Cruelty to animals and children. Her interference between husbands and wives and with their offspring made her generally detested among offenders of that type. You know as well as I do, that the way to close the breach in family relations is to intervene on behalf of one side. The wife, screaming under her husband's beating, is prepared to turn and rend anyone who dares lay a finger on the offender. Miss Tither just wouldn't learn. Again, two or three times she has brought the N.S.P.C.C. Inspector from Evingdon to investigate cases of child neglect. There have been one or two convictions on that score. I can't enumerate them all from memory, but you might look into them. Inspector Oldfield will be able to help, I'm sure. *And* the R.S.P.C.A. prosecutions, as well. There have been certain ones in that line, too. Ill-treating cattle, horses and such. She made a point of stopping and remonstrating with drunkards also, and got nothing but obscenities for her pains. But really, Inspector, do you think that any such occurrence would make one wish to murder her? The villagers have more respect for their necks, if you ask me. They have been known to fling cow-dung on her windows and one fellow fired her outhouses in revenge, but something much more serious must surely have impelled murder."

"You'd think so, wouldn't you, sir? Now, if it's not embarrassing, what about the sins you term sexual?"

"Well, ahem... well, there is the seventh commandment, which unfortunately is broken by some in the village. Not openly, of course. But a whisper here, a rumour there, then some suspicious circumstance, or even a family eruption, brings it to the light of day. Perhaps association with animals, a propinquity and familiarity with nature, shall we say, a certain laxity of speech and behaviour on the part of the froward ones, tend to lead to a light treatment of this commandment. Certainly, it does occur. Miss Tither seems to have had, to use a vulgarism, a nose for such occurrences and has interfered, to the extent, sometimes, of mentioning it to the partner sinned against. Most indiscreet and unbecoming, but it was her nature. She even tried, on occasion, to persuade me to approach and denounce the offenders, but one requires more proof than hearsay in such matters, gentlemen, or one runs a grave risk. It must almost be a case of *flagrante delicto*, and even then concerns the wronged partner and no one else. In this respect, I am firm. I am a psychologist and there my head must lead me, not my emotions."

The vicar was becoming heated and Littlejohn thought he displayed a fund of sound common sense.

"As for the rest... she, she tried to persuade certain young people that marriage was desirable in view of their relations. I was appealed to... but there again, the parties know best themselves and families have a way of settling these matters satisfactorily."

"However did she find time and develop the technique of investigation? She was a perfect vessel of wrath, wasn't she?"

"She was. She did little else than improve, or attempt to improve, the social life of the village. There, again as a psychologist, I'm afraid I must diagnose psychopathic trouble, repression causing a twisting of behaviour and purpose. Poor woman, it led her to a sad end."

Dusk was falling and the red sunset foretold a fine morrow. In distant fields, the last loads of the day's harvesting were being carried home to the farms. Noises of drivers calling to horses, children playing in the village, cattle crying, owls screeching and the notes of a few song birds broke the evening silence. The air was heavy with the smell of wood and stubble fires. Littlejohn felt hungry.

"I think I'd better be finding 'The Bell', Oldfield," he said to his colleague. "What time's dinner?"

"About seven. You'll just have time to call for a word with the Tither's maid, if you like. Then, I must be off. The inquest is to-morrow and I've a lot to do yet, although there'll be an adjournment."

The man was a perfect slave-driver, thought Littlejohn pleasantly. They bade the vicar good-night.

"I'll call again to-morrow," added Littlejohn as they parted. "Meanwhile, will you try to remember some of the severe cases of interference by Miss Tither in the private lives of people, and let me know, sir? It may prove useful."

"I certainly will, Inspector. And *do* please call on me whenever you like. Nothing is too much trouble to bring an end to this ghastly business. Good-night to you both."

On their way to Briar Cottage, the officers halted at the village police station and disturbed P.C. Harriwinckle at his evening meal of chitterlings. Whenever any of the local farmers killed a pig, a parcel of such delicacies arrived at the local police-house, for The Law was extremely partial to them. The constable had been tackling this epicurean treat in his shirt sleeves and hastily assumed his tunic to greet his superiors. Oldfield introduced the man from Scotland Yard. Harriwinckle's face glowed with pride. The thought of collaboration with the great flattered him. He could hardly wait for an opportunity of dropping-in at "The Bell" to let the village know that he and Scotland Yard were on the case. He could not, of course, be seen drinking ale with the local topers, but would call about the black-out or the like and pass an apparently casual remark.

"We'll be seeing quite a lot of each other, Harriwinckle," said Littlejohn. "We'll get together and discuss the case to-morrow and you must tell me your own views. Inspector Oldfield has already given me the official report, but I'd like to hear it again from you, verbally. Meanwhile, get on with your meal. I'm sorry we disturbed you so late. Good-night."

P.C. Harriwinckle's tunic buttons were subjected to a great strain, for his chest swelled with pride. As he disposed of his chitterlings, he rehearsed his part for the landlord of "The Bell". Casually, of course, he'd say, "And the Scotland Yard man, he sez to me, Sam, he sez, Sam, I wants your report werbal, see. Werbal, becoss I walues your report." The Law of Hilary had never had a murder on his hands before, to say nothing of a Scotland Yard colleague. Such events called for something more than tea with his pork entrails. "Mar," he yelled to his wife, "Mar, jest bring me in one o' them bottles of ale from the cell. Here's a charnct to shine come my way at last. May mean stripes fer me, 'oo knows? Now be quick about it, duck, I've work to do yet." The admiring duck forthwith waddled to the cool, barred cubby-hole, which, in the absence of malefactors in the district, was used for storing beer, rhubarb wine, pickles and next week's washing.

Meanwhile, the detectives had reached Briar Cottage. Oldfield paused at the gate. "It's getting on in the day and I've a lot to do," he said. "Mind if I leave you to this job alone and see you again in the morning?"

"Not at all. I'll just have a word or two with Sarah Russell and then I'll be after some dinner myself. I'll let you know if anything turns up."

The officers parted and Littlejohn rang the door-bell of the house. After a pause, the door opened and in the darkness beyond, for black-out regulations were here being strictly adhered to, he made out the shape of a dumpy, rotund woman, like a robust sack, tied up in the middle.

"What might you be wantin', sir?" said a pleasant country voice.

"Are you Miss Russell?"

"That's me, sir."

"May I come in? I want a word or two with you."

"What name, please?"

"Littlejohn. Inspector Littlejohn."

There was a sharp intake of breath.

"You're sure you wouldn't be wantin' to see the Rev. Wynyard, who's just arrived? He's in the dining-room 'avin' his meal."

"No, Sarah, it's you I want to see."

"Come in then, sir, although I'll have to ask you to come in the kitchen. That's the only other room blacked-out except the dinin'-room."

Littlejohn followed the woman through a dark passage and she opened a door, emitting a glow of warm, comfortable lamplight. The remnants of a meal of beef, cheese, pickles and seed-cake littered the table and sitting in a rocking-chair beside the bright fire was a visitor. He was a small, wiry man, with a heavy, sallow face, folded in the cheeks. Sparse brown hair, brushed from the side across a thinning pate. Slightly bulging, green eyes, with bilious whites. Pale, bulbous nose with narrow, twitching nostrils and below it, a thin, scattered, sandy moustache covering a wide, narrow-lipped mouth. He was perching possessively and in a most self-satisfied posture, with his large, knotted hands folded over his stomach. He glanced at the entering detective with a self-righteous superiority often found in those who fancy themselves the chosen of God.

"This is Mr. Thornbush, my 'usband-to-be; Inspector Littlejohn, this is, Walter."

Ah! the shepherd and faithful swain, thought Littlejohn to himself. Rising, Mr. Thornbush extended a limp hand and pumped that of the detective enthusiastically.

"Pleestermeetcher, friend," he said with unction.

"You can speak before Mr. Thornbush, sir. We've no secrets from each other," said Sarah, blushing.

Mr. Thornbush gravely nodded his assent, and composed himself to listen. The servant brought out a chair for Littlejohn and seated herself. She had a pleasant, round, red face, with a ready smile and her style of parting her black hair in the middle gave her a dignity of countenance quite unlike that of her chosen partner. A middle-aged, homely, worthy woman, thought the detective and worth somebody better than the self-satisfied wheelwright rocking contentedly beside him, and now and then, noisily intaking his breath as though drinking some invisible liquid.

"Well, Sarah," began Littlejohn, "I'm down here to investigate the death and bring to justice, if I can, the murderer of your late mistress…"

"Let the ungodly fall into their own nets…" interjected Mr. Thornbush to himself, as though commencing a running commentary on Littlejohn's narrative. The Inspector remembered Mr. Claplady's remarks on the shepherd's knowledge of the Psalms and resigned himself to an accompaniment of sounding brass and tinkling cymbals.

"Living with her, I'm sure you were familiar with her movements and interests," continued Littlejohn, preparing himself for the interjections from Mr. Thornbush's repertory and determined to concentrate on Sarah. "Perhaps you can tell me something about her and her activities during the last few days, up to the time of her unhappy death?"

"O, how suddenly do they consume; perish and come to a fearful end!"

Sarah shuddered at the startling intrusion. "Well, sir," she said, "I'm sure I want to help all I can. Perhaps I can tell you something that will throw light on matters. I didn't, o' course, know what was a-goin' on in Miss Tither's mind and only by what she let drop now and then, when talkin' to herself or when excited, can I say where she went. She was a deep one and kept her own counsel most times…"

"Deep calleth unto deep at the noise of thy waterspouts!"

"… Of late, she's bin very disturbed about somethin'. She came 'ome from church last Sunday mornin' and didn't want any dinner, though I'd prepared a nice cold joint, me having objections to cookin' on the Lord's Day, like."

"Remember the Sabbath Day to keep it holy!"

"What was the cause, do you think, Sarah?"

"Well, she did say somethin' about Mr. Lorrimer at Holly Bank—that's a biggish 'ouse just between the two Hilarys—havin' told her some startling news after church. It was something about the missionaries and Mr. Wynyard, I'm sure, because she was rummaging about finding the reverend's present address on account of wantin' to write to him, which she did. I posted the letter later in the afternoon."

"That's interesting, Sarah. I must look into that. I'll talk to Mr. Wynyard before I leave. Perhaps he can explain it. Anything else?"

"Well, she did get excited about somethin' else last Friday, too. As I was passin' her room upstairs, she was puttin' on her gloves to go out and a-sayin' to herself, 'Polly Druce, indeed. The little Jezebel. I'll settle Miss Druce!' Polly's a kitchen maid at the 'all and a bit of a flighty one. I should think Miss Tither was off to the 'all to see her, though she said nothing to me about it. For some time, she's been quiet like, as though not worried by other people's sins..."

"Thou puttest away all the ungodly of the earth like dross..."

"... Other people's sins, I say," went on Sarah with an admiring glance at the interjector, who by this time with his irrelevancies, was getting on Littlejohn's nerves. "Then suddenly somethin' like this happens. Two or three at a time, as you might say. Saturday, too, she had somethin' on her mind about Upper Hilary Farm. That's Mister Weekes's place. Mrs. Weekes gives her crab-apples for jelly every autumn. Powerful fine crabs they grows there. Well, Miss Tither was off with her big basket for them apples and as she goes out she sez to me, 'I'm going for my crabs,' just like that, and then, 'Would that it were only crab-apples that are bitter at Upper Hilary Farm.' Now what could she mean? Somethin' funny, I'll be bound."

"Thou hast set our misdeeds before thee; and our secret sins in the light of thy countenance."

Littlejohn controlled himself with difficulty. He longed to silence the sounding brass with caustic relish, but deemed it prudent not to upset the worthy Sarah.

Just then, the front door banged,

"Oh dear," said the servant. "That'll be Mr. Wynyard finished his supper and gone out, and you wantin' to be seeing him, sir. I'm very sorry. I ought to a' told him."

"Don't worry, Sarah. That will do to-morrow. I think I'll be going myself. What you've told me is most helpful. I will follow up one or two lines on the strength of what you say, and perhaps I'll call again when you're less occupied with your own affairs." He glanced at Thornbush, who did not quail, however, lost as he was in his own meditations.

The Inspector rose and took up his hat.

"I hope you'll benefit under Miss Tither's Will, Sarah, and be very happy in the future. You have, from all accounts, been a very faithful servant."

"That's good of you, sir. Yes, Miss Tither did say she'd not forget me, and Miss Martha who died some year or two gone, left me a somethin', too, though Miss Ethel had control of it, which did much to keep me with her. Life wasn't too easy now and agen of late. I'd everythin' to do myself, cleanin', cookin' and washin' in this big house…"

"Moab is my washpot…" came from the rocking-chair.

"But from what Miss Ethel said, they'd been very generous. I do know Miss Martha was. She was the kindest lady in the world. Left me very comfortable, provided I stayed with Miss Ethel for life."

"Blessed be the Lord, who hath pleasure in the prosperity of his servant," came the first relevant word from the Psalmody.

Littlejohn extended his hand to the maid. She shook it timidly.

"Many thanks, and good-night, Sarah."

"Good-night, Inspector, and come again if I can help you."

"I will. Good-night, Mr. Thornbush. I'll leave you to your Rose of Sharon."

Littlejohn was unable to resist this final effort. Mr. Thornbush did not smile. He took it seriously, as a compliment to himself. His face showed earnest intelligence for the first time. He accompanied Littlejohn to the door as though anxious to impart a final word of wisdom to him.

"Have you seen the Light, friend?" he asked gravely. His breath was hot, like a dog's, and smelled of caraway seeds imposed on a background of pickled onions.

"No!" said Littlejohn, and hastened away to see how much dinner was left for him at "The Bell".

CHAPTER V

Eavesdropping over Dinner

I T WAS QUITE DARK WHEN LITTLEJOHN LEFT MISS TITHER'S residence, but the Bell Inn was not far and he found his way there without any difficulty. Along the road, he encountered a dark shape moving in the opposite direction and a cheery voice called out to him.

"Good-night, sir. Hope you'll be comfortable in your quarters. I jest 'ad a word with the landlord o' 'The Bell' in that respec'. Jack Noakes, his name be. He'll see you're all right, sir."

"Thanks, Harriwinckle. That's thoughtful of you. I hope he's got something good in the oven for my supper."

"Roast pork, I believe sir," called the constable, for it was from this source that he had come by his already digesting chitterlings. "You'll not be a-wantin' anythin' more from me to-night?"

"No thanks, Harriwinckle. I'll see you to-morrow. Good-night to you."

"Good-night, sir."

"The Bell" is a modest, old-fashioned place, with little accommodation for lodgers, but as a favour to the police, Noakes, the inn-keeper, had turned his private sitting-room into a sanctum for the Inspector. Littlejohn entered the dark vestibule, passed the bar-parlour, where business for the night was just warming-up, and was greeted at the foot of the stairs by Mrs. Noakes, who led him at once to the cosy little room next door to the bar-parlour. A table was already laid for dinner there. As he waited for his meal, Littlejohn cast his eyes round the place. In the wall between his quarters and the public room, was a small hatch with a sliding door. On special occasions, such as weddings or small private functions, it was the custom of Noakes to let off his own sitting-room, and refreshment from the bar was passed through the hatch. From his place at the table, Littlejohn could hear the buzz of conversation in the parlour, but it was incoherent and confused. Miss Tither's murder had shaken the whole district and probably would be the topic of most of the chatter which accompanies evening pints of ale. The Inspector rose, softly crossed to the panel of the hatch and gently eased it open, a mere inch or so, not enough to be noticed, but sufficient to let in more sound. He found his experiment successful and his guess that Miss Tither's name would be bandied about over pots and glasses was confirmed.

Littlejohn, as he ate his supper, heard the clatter of glasses, the opening and closing of the door, the greetings as one after another joined the party, the knocking for refills, the tramp of feet. Conversation ebbed and flowed, but as soon as the murder was mentioned, there was a hush as the rest listened eagerly for news. The detective's imagination rather ran riot as voice after voice joined in. Gruff voices, thin voices, squeaky, rumbling, oily, wary, diffident, self-important, bashful voices, took up the tale. It was strange to hear the witnesses and try to judge by tone and expression whether they were reliable or not.

A loud tenor voice, it was that of Luke Pearson, an irrepressible singer in the church choir, was much in evidence as Littlejohn ate his pork and apple sauce.

"As fur as I can gather,—an' I bin rown the village to-day—nobody see Miss Tither h'after she left ole Haxley. Now, where wuz she, meanwhile? Nubbudy seems to know thaat," said the tenor.

There was a chorus of noise, which reminded Littlejohn of sounds reported by House of Commons pressmen as "Cheers".

From the chorus emerged a shriller tenor, like one taking up an aria.

"No, Luke, I got one up on yew there. My Mary saw owld Tither after her left Haxley. My gel wuz takin' up some drinks to Half-Acre, where they wuz a-reapin' and she see Miss Tither leave Haxley and go along the 'edge-bottom as though she might be makin' for the highroad to Evingdon. Our Mary says she wouldn't a' noticed it, but jest as Miss Tither leaves Old Haxley, 'er must a' put up a rabbit a-settin' there in the 'edge, and owld Haxley up with his gun and bowls 'im over, roight under Old Tither's nose. 'Er did jump, my Mary sez, and din't owld Haxley laugh."

"Well, where did 'er go to after that? That be the mystery and the puzzle," chimed in a baritone voice. The chorus took up the theme again.

The loud tenor, no doubt fortified by another half-pint, grew jocular.

"Like as not, it wuz bible-punchin' Walter, owld Thornbush, as dun it. Got sick o' waitin' for Sarah Russell's little fortune, so speeded up the course o' nature…"

Loud laughter greeted this sally.

A deep bass voice could be heard saying that Walter couldn't murder a rice pudding. The laughter was renewed.

"Naw, you'm wrong there, Jude," squeaked the voice of some ancient or other, almost a treble with age. "Thornbush be cunnin' and well able to moind 'is own interests, psalm-singin' or no psalm-singin'. There be crewelty in Walter's face, and scancti-monyussness 'ides a nasty naycher. I well remembers Walter as a boy. Proper torment 'e wuz to the gells, pulling their pigtails and the loike. A narsty little bit o' work. Then 'The Light' dawned on 'im. Or so he sez. H'ambition it wuz wot brought 'im to The Light, not an 'umble and contrite heart."

The deep bass, evidently well in liquor by this, airily dismissed the discussion.

"Come to that, well nigh everybody in the Hilarys 'ad some reason or other fer wantin' Tither out of the way. Too many secrets she knew, too dangerous loike. Proper game o' sortin'-out the police is goin' to 'ave. Same again, Jack."

There was a noise of pumping and flowing beer.

Another tenor, hitherto unheard, took up the solo part.

"Yew spoke the trewth there, 'enery. Well do oi remember the to-do we did 'ave about moi Nancy and Reuben Beallot. Reuben did say at the toime as he'd do fer Old Tither, but o' course, that wuz in the 'eat of the moment. He wuz taken up about 'aving the law on 'er, however, but Sam Harriwinckle telled 'im not to waste his money. Tither spreads it round that my Nancy and Rube wuz carryin'-on, loike, and she'd seen 'em in Pochin's spin-ney compromizin', loike. Well, as I sez at the toime, if a feller can't be compromizin' with the gel he's tokened to, who can he be compromizin' with? Jest loike that, I sez it. Nancy and Rube wuz wed not long after that. No doubt, Miss Tither speeded 'em up a bit. I'm not a grandaddy yet, though they bin wedded these two year and that's not fer owld Tither's lack of imaginin', oi'll be bound."

The voice was drowned in a pot of ale, and loud roars followed the joke.

Littlejohn, now at the cheese stage, smiled to himself. He was enjoying the entertainment and gathering information, too. He kept an old envelope at his elbow and scrawled on it from time to time.

A thick voice chimed in over the laughter.

"Many's the one as owes the Tither woman repayment. Look at the Reverend Oker. Disgraced in the eyes o' the whole congregation. Not that oi 'olds with Wesleyans at any time…"

"Whatever else you 'olds, 'old yer tongue about Wesleyans," snarled someone, evidently of the denomination.

"Now, now, no religious wars," said the landlord and guffaws rang round.

More calls for refills, knocking on the counter, the clink of coins, the flop-flop of darts, the hum of small-talk and the confusion of general conversation.

"Inquest ter-morrer,… Scotland Yard man 'ere,… Sam Harriwinckle loike a dog with two tails, he be,… jest been in 'ere swankin' about workin' hand-in-glove with a chap from London…"

The tenor was at it again.

"Pest or no pest, Miss Tither represented the peaceable citizens and, as such, we'm on 'er side agenst whomever's done 'er in, aren't we? Maybe, any one of us might be done-in next. It's up to us help catch the killer."

A chorus of approvals. Pots were knocked on the table.

The door opened and closed and heavily nailed hooves seemed to clatter into the room. There were shouts of greeting to the newcomer.

"Evenin', Isaiah, where you bin? Thowt you'd bin and got yerself murdered loike…"

Ah, thought Littlejohn, enter the man of the moment. Gormley, the first on the scene of the crime.

Isaiah was cantankerous.

"Pint o' mild and put it on the slate," he grunted.

"Where you bin?" persisted the tenor.

"I bin argewing with mi blarsted family, that's wot oi bin doin'. It's round the village as Owld Tither wuz drownded in the cesspit. An' come to think about it, too, wen oi found 'er, there wuz watter in the pit. But wen I lef' the cesspool, it wuz dry. I drained off the watter and dried 'im by shovelling out the muck from the bottom…"

"More water run in while you wuz away…" said someone jovially.

Gormley's voice grew angry.

"That's wot our George bin sayin' and we bin argufyin', till oi towld 'im to shut-up and not speak to his father loike that. Oi tell 'ee, oi turned off the inlet to the tank till oi'd cleaned 'im up and when the vicar gets moi dander up by interferin' and oi goes on stroike like, oi ups and off in temper and fergets to turn on the inflow. No. Sombody wot throwed Tither in the pit, turned on the watter, too."

There was a chorus of contention again, with Gormley's voice rising shrilly, only to be superseded by the more powerful tenor of Luke Pearson.

"Oh, put a sock in your murder talk! Oi be fed up with it. 'Ere we be, gatherin' fer a social hour, and nothing but talk o' murder to entertain us. Oi be off 'ome unless you lays off it."

This was greeted with general approval and darts became the topic of discussion. It appeared that a team from "The Bell" was shortly due to meet one from "The Bull's Head" at nearby Graby in a match to death.

Littlejohn rose and strolled into the bar parlour to size-up the gathering and establish friendly relations. He drank a pint of ale standing at the counter and was civilly greeted and treated by the assembly, now hotly enumerating the pros and cons of various aspirants for glory at darts. A reserve fell over the customers and Littlejohn decided he had better leave well alone until he was better known. He bade them good-night and wandered outside for a breath of air before retiring.

The roads were deserted. The shapes of clustered cottages could just be discerned in the pitch darkness. The wind hissed in the leaves of the trees round the inn. A fox barked somewhere in the distance and was answered by the challenges of yard-dogs. The detective lit his pipe and strolled slowly along the road. There was a scuffling of wild things in the ditches as he passed. The church clock struck ten and the regulars of "The Bell" began to turn out. Good-nights were bandied and foot-steps rang out. Crisp feet. Unsteady, staggering, shambling feet. The clink of hobnails, the pad-pad of rubbers. Here and there a torch twinkled. The Inspector retraced his steps past the few cottages clustered round the pub. Slits of dim light showed round the blinds of some; others were in darkness. A woman's shrill laughter sounded. A child wailed in one of the houses. A drunkard's angry shouts echoed; no doubt a protest at the reception he was receiving at home. Littlejohn in imagination saw Miss Tither on such a night as this. Creeping, peering, listening. An ideal night for a murder under cover of the blackness, yet someone chose to do her to death in the full light of day.

Noakes, landlord of "The Bell", was washing glasses when his guest returned. Littlejohn stopped to speak to him. They exchanged generalities. Then, "Who was the Rev. Oker?" asked Littlejohn. Noakes wiped beer-slops from the long deal table of the bar parlour and gave the detective a keen glance. The landlord was a middle-aged man, red-faced, thick-set and with pale, watery, good-natured eyes.

"Mr. Oker? Oh, he was the minister on circuit in Evingdon, but he served four churches round here. He lived between here and Evingdon and he used to come 'ere one Sunday in four takin' the services."

"What made him leave?"

"There wuz a proper shemozzle at the chapel here. Rumours got around that he was sweet on Mrs. Tandelette. The congregation fell off, hardly anybody went to service. They did say Miss Tither started the tale."

"Who was Mrs. Tandelette?"

"Wife of a Major Tandelette, a retired man who lived here, who was called-up when war broke out. He went off somewheres, leavin' his wife in the cottage—with the maid, of course. They lived at Woodbine Cottage, just past the vicarage."

"What happened?"

"Well, it seems somebody let Major Tandelette know what was goin' on. He wuz a friend of the vicar, so Mr. Claplady can tell you more about it. I don't know the details. But the Rev. Oker left the district."

"What were the rumours?"

"Mr. Oker wuz a special constable and it wuz rumoured as he was callin' too often at the cottage on his beat. That's all I can tell you."

Noakes was evidently uncomfortable and Littlejohn decided to defer matters until he could see the vicar himself. He bade the landlord good-night and retired to his room. Before he turned-in, he wrote in his notebook a summary of points for the next day.

Mr. Claplady. Query Miss T.'s activities. Any more enemies? Ask about affair of Reuben Beallot. What are true facts of the Oker-Tandelette scandal? Pursue I. Gormley's statement *re* water in cesspool. How does the contraption work?

Haxley. Movements on day of crime. Alibi? What did he discuss with Miss T. before her death? Where did she go when she left him? Who is "our Mary" who saw Miss T. after she left Haxley?

Wynyard. What did Miss T. write to him about and why was she so upset on his account? Alibi?

Lorrimer, of Holly Bank. What did he tell Miss T. after service last Sunday and why was she so perturbed?

Sarah Russell and W. Thornbush. Alibis?

Polly Druce. What was Miss T. concerned with here?

Weekes, of Upper Hilary Farm. What was the bitterness of
which Miss T. spoke and how did it concern her?

Littlejohn was just adding Home Gospel Alliance for Bringing
Sinners to Repentance to his list, when he decided that the sooner
he had that institution looked-up the better. He accordingly went
downstairs to the telephone and left a message with Scotland Yard,
that Sergeant Cromwell, his colleague, must make enquiries as
soon as possible.

Littlejohn returned quietly to his room and before long put
out the light and drew back the curtains. Heavy footsteps sounded
along the road and, as they passed, the detective made out the
broad hat and heavy silhouette of Athelstan Wynyard heading for
his lodging at Miss Tither's old home. He seemed to be returning from the vicarage. How did this man from the South Seas fit
in the strange pattern which now lay, like the pieces of a jigsaw
puzzle, awaiting arrangement and solution?

With a yawn the detective took to his bed and slept soundly
until morning.

CHAPTER VI

Mr. Claplady Collaborates

THE REV. ETHELRED CLAPLADY IS A DISTINGUISHED APIARIST and had, for five years previous to the death of Miss Tither, been engaged in writing an encyclopaedic work on his speciality. As Littlejohn neared the vicarage on the morning after his arrival in Hilary Magna, the loud metallic droning of angry bees assailed him and he gazed about him to see whence it came. His ears led him to the old, lichen-covered wall of the parson's garden and, peeping over it, he saw a strange sight. The vicar, a grotesque figure in a long, black veil suspended from an old shovel hat, and wearing gloves, was alternately puffing smoke from a pair of apiarist's bellows and stroking with the help of a feather, furious bees from the sections of honeycomb which he was carefully taking from the hives. The place was thick with the outraged insects, which, in their anger at the ravaging of their stores, had apparently accelerated the speed of their flight and swooped around the busy clergyman like fighter aircraft attacking a quarry.

The vicar spotted his audience and called out to him.

"Ah, good morning, Inspector," came thickly through the funereal gauze which muffled the gentle face. "You find me occupied for the moment, but I won't be long. No, I won't be long. I'm on the last hive."

Whereat, the better to make himself heard and with a gesture of welcome, the good man approached Littlejohn, followed by a retinue of revenging bees of which, swathed in his protective gear, the vicar seemed blissfully unaware. The detective withdrew a pace or two.

"Oh, I forgot the bees following. They're a bit angrier than usual this morning. We generally get on well together, but it's the weather that has put them out of temper. I'd suggest that you go inside and await me in my study. I'll only be about five minutes. Or, if you'd care to join me here, Mrs. Jackson, my housekeeper, will find you a spare veil and gloves."

"I'll wait in the study, sir," came the hurried reply and, noting that the disturbed insects were increasing the radius of their offensive sweeps, Littlejohn beat a hasty retreat indoors. There he was conducted to the study by a buxom, middle-aged coun-trywoman, Mr. Claplady's housekeeper. Even in the book-lined room, two or three stray insects were ominously buzzing round and beating themselves against the window-panes in their efforts to get out and resume hostilities. The Inspector speedily opened the casement and, with the help of a copy of *The Times*, assisted the intruders into the open air.

When at length the vicar arrived, he treated his visitor to a brief lecture on bees and a glass of sherry. The latter was of excellent, dry flavour and, when complimented on it, the parson flushed with pleasure and said he got it from the village stores, Mr. Allnutt, the owner of which had a pretty taste in wines himself.

"Well, sir, now to business," said Littlejohn, and the vicar grew solemn and businesslike.

"I seem, from one source or another, to have got a pretty good picture of Miss Tither's activities and unhealthy curiosity. I've accumulated, too, a list of many people who might have been affected by her poking and prying. I'll just run through the names I've heard about and, if it's not a breach of trust, which, of course I wouldn't expect you to make, perhaps you'll tell me something about them, if you can."

Littlejohn opened his notebook and scanned the list which he had scribbled there the night before.

"Reuben Beallot. Now, at the Bell Inn last night, I overheard someone say that Beallot, whoever he is, threatened to 'do for' Miss Tither over some scandal she put out about his relations with a certain Nancy. I ought to add, that it was Nancy's father who, perhaps loosed-up, shall we say, with ale, made a joke of it. All the same, it seems relevant…"

"Oh, tut, tut, tut, Inspector. Young Beallot was a farm labourer at Pochin's Farm until he was called up for the army. He's somewhere in Scotland now, I believe. A nice boy, but red-headed and hot-tempered. He was engaged to Nancy Pearce four years before they wed. Saving-up all the time for a home, you know. Miss Tither must have caught them love-making somewhere, for she came to me and tried to enlist my help in marrying them forthwith. When I told her it was not in my province and pointed out that it wasn't her business either, but that of the parties concerned, she had the impudence to go to Nancy's father. Old Pearce is a blunt countryman and gave her short shrift, but Reuben took it badly. It all blew over and they were married at the church here, in course of time. I'm certain he's not been on leave for the last four months and had he been in the village at the time of the crime, I'd be sure to know. No, Inspector, put young Beallot out of your mind. The lad's all right and has an alibi, in that he couldn't desert from his regiment without making a fuss."

"Then," went on the Inspector, again consulting his notebook, "there's the case of Mrs. Tandelette and Mr. Oker. I overheard something about that, too. What exactly happened?"

Mr. Claplady shuffled uneasily in his chair. He was more at home on the subjects of bees and theoretical psychology. The raking over of village quarrels and affairs didn't appeal to his taste at all. However, he saw his duty plainly and did his best to collaborate with the law.

"Mr. Oker was the dissenting minister here and served about four small churches in his district. He lived within the boundary of Hilary and, poor chap, doing his best when war broke out, volunteered as a Special Constable. He patrolled the roads, assisting Harriwinckle on certain nights. During the winter, Mrs. Tandelette must have seen him prowling round and looking half-starved and invited him in her cottage for a cup of coffee now and then. There was nothing wrong in that, considering there was a maid in the house, although her husband was away with his regiment. She was a very attractive woman, though, and, as usual, beauty seems to excite suspicion in women of a certain type—I might, with due respect, call it the Titherian type—ahem. Mrs. Tandelette was rather too modern for this village both in dress and a certain almost offensive forthrightness of speech. Tongues started to wag, there was scandalous talk and next time Tandelette came over on leave, Miss Tither had the audacity to mention it to him."

"How did it affect Mr. Oker?"

"Well, you see, his small congregation here has most rigid, almost prudish views, and forthwith ceased to attend. Not only that, his conduct was called to book at the general meeting of the principal church in the circuit. He showed fight and gave an admirable account of himself, I gather. He resigned then and there, too, saying such a stiff-necked congregation was no place for him. He moved to a better place somewhere near Ripon, I think. Colonel Tandelette was furious, however. He set about tracing the source of the rumour and it soon led him to Miss Tither. Before leaving for Northern Ireland, where his regiment had lately been moved, and taking his wife with him, he told Miss Tither that he wouldn't forget her share in this affair and that for two pins he'd stop her mouth for good."

The vicar regarded the detective closely.

"Now don't misunderstand me, Mr. Littlejohn. Tandelette hadn't murder in mind. He was a close friend of mine when he was here. A good chess player who regularly called and took a good beating like a gentleman. He referred to going to law, not killing the culprit."

"So, you think we can dismiss him, too?"

"By all means, by all means. The thing's unthinkable."

"Now, sir, can you tell me anything about Polly Druce?" The vicar grew pink and looked embarrassed.

"Oh dear, oh dear, will it never end? Where does Polly come in?"

"Apparently Miss Tither, as reported by her maid, left for Hilary Hall a day or two ago to deal with Polly. What would that be about?"

"I'm afraid she's a most immoral girl. She comes of a pagan family, with some gipsy blood in her. Her father is a farm labourer and a good one, too, but a more blasphemous, incorrigible reprobate I never knew. He never keeps a job for long at once, through quarrelling with his masters. Polly is a very attractive girl and clever too.

She aims rather higher than the other village girls and has a certain charm lacking in the rest of her family. She's in the kitchen at the Hall. She's been there about six months and, since she was taken on, seems to have quietened down. Lady Winstanley gave her the job and a good talking-to in an effort to reform her. Last week, Miss Tither told me she'd broken out again. Apparently she'd seen her out in the dusk with some middle-aged, married man of the village."

"Who?" interposed Littlejohn.

"Oh dear, this is so like scandalmongering! I feel tainted by discussing it. Well, I suppose you must know one way or another. It was Mr. Weekes, of Upper Hilary Farm. A more unlikely man I couldn't imagine. Mind you, I've no proof. Only Miss Tither's talk. She wanted me to intervene and I refused, so she said she would go right away to the Hall, tell Polly that unless it ceased at once, she'd denounce her to Lady Winstanley, and, furthermore, she intended telling Mr. Weekes he ought to know better."

"Who is this Weekes?"

"Ah, there is a human story, far stranger than fiction, indeed, Inspector. You know, Mr. Littlejohn, when we read certain stories in books, they are such strong meat, shall we say, that we remind ourselves that they are fiction and written for our entertainment, just as in dreams of a horrible type, we find ourselves saying strangely, 'I'm dreaming this'. But some human documents are stronger stuff than any fiction. Here is one for you. Edward Weekes and his wife, Annie, were born in this village. Until they reached forty, one was a confirmed bachelor and the other a potential old maid. Weekes was a farm foreman; she was housekeeper to an elderly retired gentleman. One month, I gather—and this from Sir Francis Winstanley—they were just nodding acquaintances; the next, they were married. You see, Warren Farm, the richest in the district, had come vacant and the pair of them had pooled their resources, made a business partnership of it, borrowed the rest of the money and taken over the farm. They made a good job of it, too, and in twenty years retired with a considerable fortune to Upper Hilary Farm, a small, comfortable place with about fifty acres or so. Have another glass of sherry, Inspector?"

The vicar, now glowing under his narrative, refilled the glasses, and resumed.

"That is the façade as shown to the world. What has gone on behind is grim. As vicar, I hear a lot that others don't. The doctor relaxes with me and, of course, I often smoke a pipe and have a yarn with Sir Francis about things in general. This is what I gather from here and there. The Weekes don't worship in the village. They attend a very strict meeting at Zion Chapel, in Evingdon. They're Calvinists to the bone and she's more rigid than he. Their natures and physiques probably account for the differences in temperament. He's a big, heavy, John-Bullish type, ready for a joke and a chat in moderation and open-handed and generous when she's not about. Or rather, he *was*. Mrs. Weekes is a little, thin, stringy woman, with a sour face, a confirmed assurance that she's one of the Elect, and a very parsimonious nature. Between ourselves, I'd be inclined to call her a married virgin. She fancies she's married beneath her, too, and likes to remind Weekes, from time to time, that whereas his father was a farm labourer and died the same, her's was head gardener on the estate and retired on his savings."

Mr. Claplady took a sip of his sherry, rolled it round his mouth with added appreciation on account of Littlejohn's praise of it, paused as though creating dramatic suspense, and continued.

"Now here's the horror of it all. Weekes's father and several other members of the family drank themselves to death. There's alcoholic taint in the blood and Weekes seeing so much of it and fortified by the Calvinism he's embraced, remains strictly total-abstainer until, suffering from nervous trouble, which gives him insomnia, he's advised by an old-fashioned doctor, Drawbell of Evingdon, to take a toddy of whisky just before bed. You can well imagine why he develops nerve trouble. He lives with a woman who's never been a wife in the real sense. He's a full-blooded, open-air man and suffers the lusts of the flesh like his fellows, but these he exorcises with the help of St. Paul, shall we say, and doses of Calvin. Whilst he's actively farming The Warren, with farm lads living in with them and interesting work from morn to set of sun, he's right enough. But, when he comes to retire, in the late fifties, to a lonely little farm, with no hands or servants about, ah, then the flesh begins to torment him. Imagine, night after night, sitting there, as I've seen the pair of them when I've had occasion to make an evening call. The lamp in the middle of the table, a ring of brightness, and dark outside it and, on each side, Weekes and Annie, she reading the Bible, he pretending to do the same perhaps, but wrestling with the flesh and images that won't be gainsaid. And the stillness of the place. Yes, and the boredom and perhaps even hate. The situation would drive me mad in a week."

The good man shuddered and pointed a dramatic finger at Littlejohn.

"But here's the climax. When Drawbell prescribed whisky, Mrs. Weekes must have known what would happen. There's only one end to breaking the pledge with a history like that of Edward's family. Yet—and Codrington, the local G.P., who's a crony of mine, tells me this—yet, she allowed it, religious scruples or no religious scruples. Nay, she encouraged it. Now, Allnutt, my warden, who supplies the stuff, confides to me that there's a case of bottles goes to Upper Hilary every week. And Codrington insists that unless it stops, and at once, Weekes'll not see another summer, from cirrhosis. Put two and two together, Inspector. Weekes has broken his bonds and yielded to the flesh. Polly Druce isn't the first. Mrs. Weekes has found out. So... the way of transgressors is hard. Very hard. So is she. She's killing him by allowing, nay, perhaps plying, the whisky."

Both men sat still, the vicar sadly pondering, the detective astounded. A stray bee buzzed in the window. Outside, a scene of great animation was visible. The vicar's housekeeper was chasing chickens in a wire-netting enclosure down the garden, laden harvest-carts were sailing past, only the loads visible over the thorn hedge. The steam of a train could be seen in the far distance. The only sounds were the angry, persistent drone of the bees, the cackle of hens, the ring of someone's hone against his scythe and the tick of the large clock.

Littlejohn broke the mood.

"Miss Tither was there recently, gathering crab-apples for jelly and, incidentally, remarked in passing to Sarah, that there were more bitter things at Upper Hilary Farm than crabs. I wonder if she'd been meddling there, too?"

"I wouldn't be a bit surprised, Inspector. She was in at everything unsavoury in the locality."

"I must call and see the Weekes pair sometime. And now, there's another couple of characters in the case. Mr. Lorrimer, of Holly Bank, and the Rev. Athelstan Wynyard, of the South Seas."

"I'm afraid I can't help you much in either case, but fire away, I'll do what I can."

"Who's Mr. Lorrimer, to begin with?"

"I really can't tell you very much about him. He came to live here about three or four years ago. A fellow of about fifty-five or sixty years of age. He's apparently very nicely off; they say he made his money in Australia or somewhere and came back to settle down in the old country. He attends service at the church on Sunday mornings and seems to lead a quiet life, not mixing very much."

"Was he friendly with Miss Tither? I ask that because, according to her maid, something he said to Miss Tither last Sunday after church disturbed her considerably and caused her to write to Mr. Wynyard."

"Ah," said the vicar and looked very uncomfortable. "May I ask you to discuss that with Mr. Wynyard himself? I'm committing no breach of confidence when I say that he called here last night in a very excited state of mind and made to me what I regard as a confession. It was a statement in private which I would prefer not to disclose without his consent. I advised him to open his heart to you, Inspector. So perhaps you'll make it in your way to see him about it."

"Certainly, sir."

"Another glass of sherry before you go?"

"No, thanks." The vicar absent-mindedly refilled his own glass and sipped it meditatively.

Littlejohn thought it time to terminate the interview. The vicar was a perfect mine of information. Littlejohn wondered if he would ever find the needle in the huge haystack which the good man had dumped on him. He decided to call on several of the characters of their discussion. Meanwhile, he had more than enough matter to begin working on. All that remained was to enquire concerning the mechanism of the cesspool. When asked to describe it, Mr. Claplady evinced signs of great distress.

"I'm sorry, Inspector, but I'm not in the least mechanical minded. I allowed myself to be persuaded, without expert guidance, when the thing was installed, by a salesman and Gormley has acted as engineer ever since, although somewhat of a crude mechanic, shall we say. He, he! Perhaps you'd care to ask him about it… or let me see… yes, I think I have them still. Yes, I think I can lay my hands on them." He proceeded to rummage intently in disorderly cupboards and drawers until, finally, he emerged, dusty yet triumphant, with a sheaf of papers which he handed to the detective. Specifications, persuasive letters, testimonials from satisfied users and, finally, a diagram of the sanitary system of the vicarage, including detailed blue-prints of the cess-tanks. Littlejohn glanced carefully at the drawings and nodded.

"May I keep these for the time being, sir? They'll probably be instructive to the Coroner at the inquest this afternoon. Which reminds me, I must be off, or I'll not be there in time, especially as I must see Inspector Oldfield about these particulars you've given me."

"By all means, keep them, Inspector. I'll see you at the inquest at which, to my distress, I'm a witness. Good morning. You'll find your way out, won't you?"

Littlejohn assured the parson that he could, and made his exit. After his departure, the vicar rose unsteadily. He had never taken three glasses of his own potent sherry before and felt strange in the legs and somewhat lightheaded. He ruminated on the interview which had just terminated. His drinks seemed to have sharpened his mind and made him feel bold. "Polly Druce is a *tart*," he solemnly told himself, as though making an astounding discovery and then, suddenly, the epithet, which in more sober moments would have brought shame to his cheeks, seemed to give him food for thought. "Ah, tart," he said with relish and peeped through the window. Mrs. Jackson was still busy in the hen-run. One of her brood had suddenly taken to eating its own eggs and she was catching the hens one by one and examining their beaks with a view to detecting the criminal. Finding her fully occupied, the vicar rose somewhat gingerly and softly entered the larder. There, in all its glory, stood a marvellous apple flan, the housekeeper's speciality and her master's weakness. "Ah, tart," said the good man again and raided the store of a large portion, which he stealthily carried back to his den. After taking a large bite, he placed the rest carefully on his blotting-pad for further attention later and, opening a drawer, took out a huge bundle of papers marked "The Life of the Bee (*Apis Mellifica*)", by Ethelred Claplady, M.A. (Cantab.). Having fumbled with the pile until he found the place where he had last ceased his writing, page 1,103, he dipped his pen in the ink, shook a blot on the carpet, took a further bite of his tart, and forgot all about the troubles of Hilary in the problems of his bee hives.

CHAPTER VII

Inquest

ONE NIGHT SOON AFTER ETHEL TITHER'S MURDER, P.C. Harriwinckle dreamed a dream. He and his wife made two great inert mounds in their capacious connubial bed and they snored lustily in concert, the trumpetings of healthy folk after a day's work well done. But if Constable Harriwinckle's huge frame was *couchant*, his mind was *rampant*. In a vision, he saw himself roving his native countryside, unravelling the threads of a crime in which the victim was alternately Miss Tither and Inspector Oldfield, and, having finally brought the criminal to justice, he received his sergeant's stripes at the hands of the Coroner, Mr. Absalom Carradine, M.B.E. As Harriwinckle's snores broke, subsided, turned to gasping whistles, and finally ceased in the process of awaking, the three silver chevrons on his sleeve miraculously changed to a higher honour in the form of a black armlet on which were inscribed in flaming scarlet, the letters M.B.E. The limb of the law opened his eyes and for a moment lay still and disgusted by the side of his partner. His disgust was due to the fact that in his dream the criminal had been formless and void, like an unfixed photograph which has faded away. A thin pencil of light filtered round the edge of the black blind of the bedroom. Outside the roosters were already challenging each other with their frantic crowing, the hens in the back garden were making the plain-tive noises which precede eggs. The ducks, having already done their duty by Mrs. Harriwinckle under cover of night, sported on the pond behind the police station, quacking merrily. P.C. Harriwinckle made up his mind.

"Mother," he said, to the torpid heap of flesh and bedclothes at his side. "Mother, I'm gettin' up. There's work to do."

Mrs. Harriwinckle continued to snore, so, having done his part by holding no secrets from her, her husband slid nimbly from beneath the blankets, gathered his clothes from the bedside chair and padded downstairs in his nightshirt and bare feet. He was fully dressed and ready for business at six o'clock, indicated by the opening and closing of the double doors of a cuckoo-clock, which Mrs. Harriwinckle's brother, Gus, a youth-hostel enthusiast, had brought home as a proof of his efforts in the Black Forest. The constable's youngest, Harry, had so thoroughly dealt with the bird during a one-time absence of his parents, that ever after, the cuckoo remained at home and marked the passing hours with unseen cries. When Harriwinckle met Littlejohn at noon, as the Inspector was leaving the vicarage, he had a good morning's work to report.

"Mornin', sir," he said, saluting genially. "I bin lookin' fer yew. Maybe, I thought, you might have some orders. So, not bein' able to foind yew, I set about gatherin' one or two alibis of folk I'd learned was about when Miss Tither was murdered."

"That's very enterprising of you, Harriwinckle. You've shown great initiative. There's a lot to do in this business and it's nice to collaborate with a willing and energetic helper."

The village constable's healthy complexion turned a deeper shade of brick-red, his chest threatened to burst his tunic-buttons and it was only with difficulty that he was able to extract from his breast pocket a dog-eared, black notebook, which, after he had disentangled it from the chain of his whistle, he opened and made as if to read at length.

Littlejohn interposed. He had no desire to stand in the middle of the road in the heat of the day, listening to a long recital.

"I know that drinking on duty's not allowed, Harriwinckle, but I suggest we go in conference in my room at 'The Bell' and sort your notes out there in private."

"With pleasure, sir, if it's all the same to yew."

"Come along then, and as we walk, tell me whom you've visited, and why."

"Well, sir. First, it's known that Mr. Haxley was one o' the last to see Miss Tither. I got a statement from 'im. Then, as Sarah Russell is reputed to be comin' into money when Miss T. dies, I thinks it as well to see where she was at the toime of the croime. I got her alibi. *And* checked it. You probably heard, too, that Mr. Thornbush reckons on marryin' Sarah now she's free. Thinkin' that it bein' to his adwantage to have Miss T. out of the way, I thinks it best to see 'im also. I got his statement in my book, too. Perhaps it was as well I saw 'im. A proper slippery eel he is, that one. Full o' texts and psalms he is, whenever in difficulty. No doubt, when you came across him last night, as he said you had, you got nothin' but psalms from 'im. That's his crafty way. He can talk proper when he wants, and I see to it that he did. 'Look you 'ere, Walter Thornbush,' says I, havin' known him since we was boys, 'look you 'ere, come down to earth a bit and ferget the heavenly language fer a while and speak in the tongue of Hilary.' Jest loike thaat, I says it, and sure enough he give me his particulars without so much as a text. Always looks as if he'd been havin' a bath in his sawdust, does Walter, when you visits him in his wheelwright's shop. Sawdust on his whiskers, chippings in his hair, shavings all over 'is clothes and fine wood-powder everywhere else. But I'm wastin' your time, sir. Then, I saw Sam Wood's daughter, Mary, who's been tellin' in the village that she saw Miss Tither after she left Mr. Haxley. I got some details from 'er, too. I think that's about the lot, sir."

"I congratulate you, Harriwinckle. You've had a busy morning and, from my angle, a very helpful one, too. Here's 'The Bell'. We'll continue over a little refreshment."

Over pints of beer, the two officers began to disentangle the mass of information contained in Harriwinckle's black book. It had been inscribed at speed and the constable's writing had assumed hieroglyphic form which he alone could translate. So, taking a sheet of paper, Littlejohn neatly jotted down the details as the policeman read them out.

Haxley. Left Miss Tither just after ten o'clock. She was apparently on her way to the main road by the field path and seemed to have time to spare. Haxley went to Home Farm after leaving Miss T. to discuss partridge shooting with Southwell, the owner. Southwell confirms that he was there from 10.30 until about noon and fixes times by kitchen clock when they went indoors for a drink.

Mary Wood, who was crossing the field and saw Miss Tither leave Haxley, who caused a commotion by shooting a rabbit almost under Miss T.'s nose. Miss T. made off along the hedge following the path at a moderate pace and Mary went on her way with drinks to the men. Uncertain about time, but thinks it was about a quarter of an hour after her mistress told her to take the drinks, remarking "Mary, get off with them drinks, quick. It's turned ten and the men will be parched".

Sarah Russell. Indoors doing housework all morning. At time of murder, say between ten and eleven, was preparing dinner. Ben Groby, jobbing gardener, who was doing his day-a-week at Miss Tither's, testifies that he saw her about the place most of the time. The scene of the crime is a good half-mile from Briar Cottage and Groby states she couldn't possibly have gone out and come back for so long without his noticing. He was burning rubbish near the kitchen and she was working there and he kept his eye on the place to see that the smoke wasn't blowing in the house.

Walter Thornbush. Greatly indignant at being questioned, as he regards himself as above suspicion. Finally, stated that he never left his shop. His apprentice, Enoch Tyson (18), a lad with plenty of commonsense, confirms this. They were finishing a hay-cart for Gasson of Poger's Dam, and, as it was a rush job, kept hard at it all morning.

"Well, Harriwinckle," said Littlejohn, laying down his pencil, emptying his tankard and stretching his long legs beneath the table, "that's a good morning's work and seems to put those you've questioned out of the running, for the time being, at least. And now, I must bestir myself and get some lunch. It's turned quarter to one and Inspector Oldfield's due here at one. We've a lot to do before the inquest, which is at two-thirty, isn't it? I guess you'll be busy too, meanwhile."

"I shall that, sir, and I'd best be goin'. I'll be seein' you at the inquest, then."

Oldfield arrived shortly after Harriwinckle's departure and found his colleague eating cold beef and pickles. They discussed the forthcoming proceedings. Oldfield was, of course, asking for an adjournment and hoped that the mere formalities of time and cause of death would be gone through and the rest left for the future. Littlejohn told Oldfield the results of his own and Harriwinckle's work in the morning and they arranged to go carefully over the scene of the crime as soon as the Coroner had been disposed of. Such disposal was, however, easier said than done.

Mr. Absalom Carradine, M.B.E., was the principal solicitor of Evingdon, and a very efficient man after his fashion. Circumstances had embittered him against the rural population, however. His son, Roger, had, some years back, confidently put up as Conservative candidate for the Evingdon division of Trentshire, a safe Tory seat for centuries. But his father's activities in matters concerning tithes had antagonized the whole agricultural labouring class against him and his family, with the result that they did not, as heretofore, vote as expected. Instead, they returned a nondescript Labour candidate and cast Roger to the bottom of the poll with such a thud, that he only barely escaped forfeiting his deposit. To make matters worse, however, at the next general election little more than a year afterwards, the disgusted Roger having withdrawn in favour of another Conservative hopeful, the labourers of Evingdon division almost unanimously ejected Mr.

Smithkins, their Socialist M.P., in favour of the Tory. Absalom Carradine never forgave that piece of impudence and whenever he encountered agricultural labourers in his courts, he gave them a gruelling. He set about Isaiah Gormley almost as soon as he had been sworn.

The Coroner's court was held in the Village Institute, a converted tithe-barn near the Bell Inn. Mr. Carradine, M.B.E., sat on a rostrum, with his clerk by his side and a large jug of brackish-looking water in front of him. He was a tall, portly man of seventy or thereabouts, with a pink, heavy face, roman nose, white hair and moustache and stern blue eyes, which shone like steel through his old-fashioned gold pince-nez. His jury sat at right-angles to him on bentwood chairs, a selection of shuffling countrymen, dressed in their best and looking overawed at the important duties which had suddenly been thrust upon them. They had inspected the body and tried to look like initiates who knew what they were about.

The room was crowded to suffocation. Inquests are rare in Hilary and all who could attend were present. Washing, shopping, baking and mending had either been crushed into a morning's work or abandoned until another day by most of the women of the place. It was harvest time, but as many casual labourers as possible had taken a half-day and, dressed in their best, jostled for seats in the Institute. The principal parties to the enquiry, the police, Mr. Claplady, Isaiah Gormley, Mr. Haxley and a few others were seated on a long bench facing the Coroner. Behind them, the rank and file snorted, whispered, tittered and sweated. One of the Gormley women had even brought a child-in-arms and when it began to whine miserably through lack of air and comfort, successfully gagged it with a large dummy-teat.

Mr. Carradine, after closely perusing a dossier on the desk before him, suddenly raised his head, stared at the audience after the fashion of a bull facing a toreador's red rag and addressed them pungently.

"This isn't an afternoon's entertainment and I won't have my court turned into a cinema show. Any more noise and I'll clear the room."

There was an awful hush, punctuated by heavy mass-breathing. Someone dropped an umbrella and recovered it with deep embarrassment, and the proceedings commenced.

P.C. Harriwinckle, hot and important, told of his share in the discovery of the body and was handled very civilly by the Coroner. He had, during the electioneering of Mr. Roger Carradine, done his best to keep law and order at his meetings and saved him a time or two from the horseplay of certain unruly elements which dogged his footsteps wherever he toured. Mr. Absalom had not forgotten it. He complimented the constable on his evidence which was briefly corroborated by Mr. Claplady and I. Gormley and then turned to Inspector Oldfield, who was primed with the more technical features of the investigation. He told how he had been notified of the crime by his subordinate and had hurried right away to Hilary. The Coroner had already viewed the scene of the murder and followed the evidence closely, making notes the while.

"Had the body been removed from the, ahem, the cesspool when you got there?"

"No, sir. The vicar was on the spot when Gormley, the labourer, found the body and saw to it that nothing was touched until we arrived."

"Very commendable of him," said Mr. Carradine soberly, deliberately omitting Gormley from his praise. "And was there anything noteworthy about the position of the corpse?"

"It was lying face downwards in about four inches of water. The hands were spread, as one does in an effort to break a fall, although the lady was unconscious when thrown-in."

"Matters relating to the autopsy are the doctor's business," snapped the Coroner. "Proceed with a description of matters as you found them."

Oldfield continued without turning a hair. He was used to this kind of treatment from Mr. Carradine, in whose courts he appeared about once a week.

"Her handbag and umbrella were under the body. An old-fashioned watch, pinned on the breast of the deceased, had stopped at eleven and a half minutes past eleven."

"H'm. Have we any reason to suppose that that was the precise time of death?"

"At first, we thought so. It has been ascertained that Miss Tither was proud of her watch and its timekeeping and checked it every morning by wireless time before the eight o'clock news was read."

"From whom was this information obtained?"

"From Sarah Russell, the maid of the deceased."

"Is she here?"

Sarah Russell was sworn, and confirmed the Inspector's statement. The officer resumed.

"A watchmaker from Evingdon has examined the watch and gives his expert opinion that its stoppage is due to water getting in the works."

"Is he here?"

With a sigh, Oldfield gave place to Theodore Lee, of Evingdon, who emphatically testified in support of the Inspector's evidence. He was so sure of himself, that Mr. Carradine reprimanded him for impertinence and sent him packing with a grievance.

"You made reservations concerning the time of death, Inspector. Why?"

"Perhaps my expression misled you, sir. May I explain? That shown by the watch was, in fact, the approximate time of death, but there is reason to believe that some time elapsed between the deceased being thrown in the tank and dying."

"How could that be?" interposed the Coroner impatiently. "You are surely not straining at the brief period of immersion necessary for drowning?"

"No, sir. But it has been suggested that at the time the body was thrown in the cesspit, there was no water in it, and it must have slowly seeped in afterwards, or alternatively been poured in."

"What nonsense is this?"

"The labourer who cleaned the pit on the morning of the crime turned off the inflow, thoroughly shovelled out the residue of filtration and left no liquid in it."

"Is the man in court?"

There was a commotion as Isaiah Gormley again presented himself for questioning. He was dressed in his best. Having only half a Sunday suit, which consisted of a green tail coat of ancient design with black tape pipings, he had borrowed a pair of trousers from his son, George Hackingsmith, which were too narrow round the waist and too long in the leg and made him walk as though mounted on horseback. He wore, too, a celluloid collar, supported by a ready-made tie, which had seen better days, and a dicky, which projected at each side. Mrs. John Henry Gormley, who sat in court, still stifling her youngest with a rubber dummy-teat, had turned him out thus and was proud of him.

The re-appearance of the ancient caused a stir in court and a concerted murmur of encouragement rose from the audience, as did the composite odour of unwashed bodies, dirty linen, stale tobacco, moth balls and liniment, which had long been struggling for mastery against the disinfectant with which the room was cleaned. The Coroner turned a baleful eye on the offenders and the hum died down like that of an organ from which the wind power has suddenly been cut off.

Gormley was accidentally sworn again and with difficulty, and faced the Coroner with a look alternating between extreme cupidity and arrested development.

"Now, Gormley, what is all this about the cesspool being quite empty?"

"It wuz, yer worship."

"But surely it would refill rapidly as the water from the house was poured down sinks and the like."

"Naw."

"Why?"

"Cos oi turned un awf at the tap."

Oldfield here interposed, placing the diagram supplied by the vicar before him.

"I see from the drawing before me that there are two tanks, one of which fills first and contains bacteria. The jury will follow closely."

The eight men tried to look wise. Mr. Carradine read the blueprint haltingly.

"The first tank deals with solid matter, which falls to the bottom and is consumed by the bacteria; the liquid drains off into the second tank through a pipe half-way up the first, and then, after filtering through a bed at the base of the second tank, passes, purified, into the ditch which carries it away. There is a stop-cock on the pipe connecting the two tanks. Do you say you closed that, Gormley, whilst you worked on the second one?"

"Yus, oi dun that."

"Stop shuffling and speak up, Gormley."

Isaiah had also borrowed a pair of his son's boots, which were a size too small for him and he was frenziedly trampling the floor to gain relief. He made as if to spit and then, remembering himself, swallowed with great agitation of his Adam's-apple.

"Now, Gormley. Had you finished the work, and closed the trap of the tank?"

"Naw. Oi dun all but put new cinders in bottom of un."

"Why did you leave the job half-way through the morning?"

"Oi went on stroike."

"You *what?*"

Mr. Carradine was beginning to enjoy himself. Such evidence of bolshevik activities was right down his street.

"Oi went on stroike," repeated the ancient with greater emphasis, gazing blankly at the large framed portrait of the donor of the Institute, the late Colonel Phillimore-Cadby, who for twenty-two years had been returned unopposed as M.P. for Evingdon and during that time had not made a single speech in the House.

"Explain yourself and remove the impudent expression from your face. This is a court, not a taproom."

There was a muffled commotion in court due to discreet mirth, indignation and the vociferous realization by Mrs. Gormley's baby that the teat was a dummy.

Old Gormley's eye fell on the clock and he suddenly realized that if he did not hurry, closing-time would be upon him. He was anticipating a lot of free pints for his share in the entertainment and, therefore, speeded up his testimony and intelligence. Before he left the box, he had, much to Mr. Claplady's discomfiture, explained the circumstances of his down-tools protest. He also stated that he had arranged with Mrs. Jackson, the vicar's house-keeper, to be sparing in her use of the drains until he had finished in the cesspit. Yes, in his dudgeon, he had walked off and left the connecting tap closed. No, he did not think at the time about the embarrassment such an act might have caused. He wasn't used to using cesspools, only to cleaning them. The Coroner roundly trounced him. He told him he was a disgrace to the village and, as an elder, ought to be setting a better example. Mr. Carradine expressed grave displeasure at Gormley's ignorant testimony, impertinence, absence of public spirit and lack of understanding of the importance of inquests. He even mentioned the grave risk Isaiah had run of being committed for contempt. Under this load of sin and wrath, the ancient creaked out of the box, winked at the audience, made his exit and had to pay for his own beer after all.

The rest of the proceedings fell rather flat after Gormley's comic interlude. Dr. Codrington gave medical evidence, which showed that death was due to drowning, but that there were severe bruises and lacerations of the head, which would have produced the necessary state of unconsciousness for the unresisted drowning in four inches of drain water. As regards the weapon which had inflicted the injuries to the head, it might have been a heavy stick, a stone, the handle to, say, a pitchfork, or even the butt-end of a gun. When cleaned, the wounds revealed the impression of being created by any of the objects mentioned. Time of death tallied approximately with that of the stopped watch. Asked by the Coroner if any other items of interest came to light at the autopsy, Dr. Codrington stated that the hands were clenched and, on forcing open the palm of the right one, he found a small, crumpled ball of paper. On examination, this proved to be one of Miss Tither's own tracts. "The Way of the Ungodly shall Perish", was printed in red ink on a white ground and across the print had been scrawled, in large blue pencil, a very obscene word, which made Mr. Carradine clear his throat as he read it.

Mr. Claplady corroborated Gormley's testimony and received a sympathetic comment from the Coroner concerning the unseemly, nay, despicable behaviour of the old labourer. Sarah Russell said she had no idea where Miss Tither was going at the time she met her death. Mr. Haxley, who caused a sensation by refusing to be sworn, stated that he had no idea where Miss Tither went after she left him. He and Mary Wood both told the tale about the shooting of the rabbit after which they left Miss Tither to her own devices.

Mr. Carradine had had quite enough of this rural inquest. The odour of the stuffy atmosphere, the bucolic faces watching his every move, the self-conscious eagerness of his jury, were getting on his nerves. He turned to his eight trusty men and told them to return a verdict of wilful murder against some person or persons unknown. The jury formally hissed in each others' faces by way of considering their problem, agreed with the Coroner, and their finding was accordingly entered.

The audience remained seated as though waiting for another turn on the bill whilst Mr. Carradine wrote-up and gathered his notes, whispered to his clerk and the police and released the jury. The gathering was broken-up by the excited arrival of a youth in corduroys who, with sublime disregard for the place in which he was intruding, rushed to Mr. Claplady and whispered in his ear.

The vicar turned to Littlejohn in great excitement.

"Oh dear, oh dear. It *would* happen just now. Please excuse me, one of my hives has swarmed!"

And gathering up his hat, the good man chased off in the direction of a black cloud which was rapidly approaching the distant horizon.

CHAPTER VIII

Topography

A S HE EMERGED FROM THE INSTITUTE AT THE TERMINATION of the inquest, Littlejohn thought to himself, "Now we can get down to business at last." Since his arrival in the village, he had accumulated a mass of disorderly information, alibis, thumb-nail sketches of personalities and details of the crime. He wished to settle down to his own orderly routine, deal with one thing at a time, and clear his mind of encumbrances. He took from his pocket a foolscap envelope which Mr. Claplady had handed to him when they met in the Coroner's court, with an injunc-tion to peruse its contents at his leisure. He found it to contain a rough map, drawn in ink on a piece of foolscap by the vicar, whose ideas of cartography were not very precise. The gesture, however, was a gracious one and the plan now in his hands would prove very useful.

Oldfield joined his colleague in the road. The villagers, still hanging round in knots, as though expecting something sen-sational to turn up, eyed the pair with eager expectation. The Inspector from Evingdon had little new in the way of informa-tion and Littlejohn was the same, but at the Scotland Yard man's suggestion, they again visited the scene of the crime. There, Littlejohn took out the vicar's map and checked his position. A triangular area of grazing land, with the village centre as its apex, constituted the spreading stage of the murder. From the

Bell Inn, one side of the triangle, consisting of the main street and the Evingdon-Stretton Harcourt Road, extended to meet the base, which was the Stretton Lattimer Road. The other side, again from the inn, travelled a crooked course to meet the base near the church and vicarage. The two buildings last mentioned were surrounded on two sides by oaks and sycamores, a pleasant sight to see; the remaining two sides of the square containing them consisted of roads. The cesspool lay in a hollow between the churchyard and the vicarage hedge. This hollow gradually rose until it reached ground-level near the thickest part of the trees. At this point, too, there began a thick, hawthorn hedge, which ran parallel to the base of the triangular field, thus cutting it in two, and terminating at the Evingdon Road. Littlejohn, with Oldfield peeping over his shoulder, took his bearings from the vicar's chart and seemed satisfied.

"A bit rough and out of proportion," commented Oldfield, "but a useful effort. There's the footpath, marked by dots." He pointed to the field-path, which began at the tip of the triangle and cut straight through the field to the vicarage side entrance, making its way through the hawthorn hedge by a short tunnel of thick foliage and branches. Half-way in its course, the path was joined by a tributary, which had its source at a stile on the Evingdon Road. Oldfield pointed to a spot mid-way along the by-path. "That's about where Miss Tither met Haxley, according to the vicar."

Littlejohn carefully filled his pipe, lit it and puffed awhile. They had strolled through the tunnel and were standing on the top side of the hawthorn hedge. The land from there rose gently and then, just before reaching the village street, flattened suddenly, thus forming a plateau, on which the roofs of cottages and the police station were just visible.

"So only the vicarage side-windows overlook the field here," he said, "and, unless someone were actually wandering about in it, the murderer could carry on unseen."

"Yes," replied Oldfield, "but he'd be running a grave risk. The vicar's house practically covers the whole view, except that just under the near side of the hedge, here. Now, that's the place where it seems most likely Miss Tither was laid-out. Then she was carried, not dragged, mind you, because we examined the ground for traces. She was carried under cover of the hedge, and through the gap and down to the pool. Unless, as you say, someone was prowling round the field, the murderer would be operating under a screen of trees practically all the way."

"Well," suggested Littlejohn, "let's try a reconstruction of the crime. Everything points to a murder, or, at least, a blow, struck under the cover of the hawthorn, as obviously it would have been the height of folly to try it in midfield, on the road, or in the church or vicarage grounds. The point is, how was she decoyed under the hedge?"

"Perhaps the murderer waved to her or called out."

"Yes. That could be, but do you remember what was found clutched in her hand?"

"The tract with the rude word scrawled across it?"

"Exactly. Could it have been used as a banner, let's say, to attract her attention? Mr. Claplady's plan is about the size of the tract which was produced to the Coroner. We'll put it on the hedge, here, and see if it's visible from the path branching to the Evingdon Road."

Littlejohn laid his white paper in the branches of a bush near the gap in the hedge and the two strolled to the spot mentioned. The map was quite visible.

"Probably the tract was placed near the spot where the path cuts the hedge. The gap there would provide cover for the murderer as he waited for his victim. Then, the blow having been struck, he'd about twenty yards to go to the cesspit. Let's look at the hedge near the place."

The two men retraced their steps and began to examine the hawthorns, now turning darker green and brown with the approach of autumn. About a yard from the gap on the Evingdon Road side, Oldfield found something.

"Here we are, Littlejohn," he said excitedly. Three broken twigs, recently snapped, revealed a projecting spike of thorn. "A good spot on which to impale the warning to the ungodly, with an added commentary," said Littlejohn.

"But, why the commentary, as you call it?"

"Just to hold her attention for a minute. Otherwise, she might just have snatched it down and carried it off before the murderer could strike."

Oldfield rubbed his chin and gazed in the direction of the cesspool.

"But why carry her to the drain, raise the cover and throw her in?"

"Perhaps the murderer saw Gormley at work there. It's visible from the Stretton Lattimer Road. He knew—and this shows he's familiar with goings-on in the village—he knew that the place was only cleaned out half-yearly. Gormley had just finished. What better hiding-place? And, in addition, the majority of such contraptions greatly increase the rate of decomposition. He might have fancied, with some justification, that before the next clean-out, the body would have almost disappeared. Gormley comes along, shovels it out with a lot of other rubbish, bears it off to the tip, and there's an end of it. Gormley's almost a half-wit and it's even chances he wouldn't have guessed what he'd unearthed. Even if the crime *did* eventually come to light and be investigated, the concealing of the body gave the murderer time to cover his tracks, recover his poise and nerve and, perhaps make an orderly and normal-looking flight. He counted without Gormley's eccentricities, however, and hence, the police are right on his heels. We mustn't let the trail get cold, Oldfield."

"The point that puzzles me, however," interposed Oldfield, "is, what was Miss Tither doin' between leaving Haxley and getting herself murdered? Where was she goin' in the first place and for what purpose? Harriwinckle's scouring the village, with little success, I'm afraid, to try to find out the answer."

As though waiting for his cue, however, the constable suddenly breasted the rise and appeared, making gestures that he had news. He joined his superior officers, almost bursting with his information and from his exertions.

"I found where Miss Tither was a-goin' on the morning she was killed, sirs," he said, gulping to recover his breath. "During the inquest, a message came over the telephone, which Mrs. Harriwinckle tuck, her always standing-by whenever I be about my business. Well, it was from Miss Satchell, as keeps the roadside tea-house at the Stretton cross-roads. She said she wanted to speak to me. So, when I gets in, I rings her up. She tells me that on the mornin' of the croime, Miss Tither called there at about half-past ten and stayed till eleven, persumably waitin' for somebody or other. Then, at eleven—Miss Satchell's sure of the time, because at eleven she starts gettin' ready for lunches—at eleven, then, Miss Tither gets awful cross, makes clickin' and snorting noises loike, and pays fer 'er coffee and offs in a temper."

"Good, Harriwinckle. I'm glad your efforts have come to somethin'," said Oldfield encouragingly, to which the constable was heard to reply that it was Miss Satchell, not himself, as earned the praise. "She said she heard of the croime yesterday, but 'twasn't till this mornin' that she realized that what she knew might be of h'importance."

"Now," said Littlejohn, "we've to find out whom she was meeting."

"Oi'm comin' to that," said Harriwinckle, now almost exploding with eagerness to get the rest of his tale off his chest. "Miss Satchell said as Miss Tither axed her as she came in, if a clergyman had been about yet, and that if she saw one on the road, to call 'im in, else tell her. Now, sirs, could that a bin the Reverend Claplady? A tall clergyman, Miss Satchell wuz told, come to think of it, though. That doesn't sound loike vicar to me. Still, he moight pass for tall in a crowd o' little uns."

"No, I think not," answered Littlejohn. "I can guess who it was. Miss Tither, according to the maid, Russell, wrote to a clergyman on Sunday and posted the letter. I think we'll find it was Mr. Wynyard she was expecting."

"Well, I'll be dashed!" said Oldfield. "Things are warming up."

They explained to the bewildered Harriwinckle who Mr. Wynyard was.

"I think the reverend gentleman is the next on the agenda and we'll find him at Briar Cottage, where he's now camping," said Littlejohn.

"We'd better not both go," suggested Oldfield. "Might scare him into complete silence. I'll be getting back to Evingdon. I've lots to do. Let me know if there's any other way I can help."

Before parting, the three men examined the gap in the hawthorn hedge for any traces which might have been overlooked. Livestock had used the whole neighbourhood pretty freely and all the searchers found were the hoof-marks and droppings of cows and a confused mass of horseshoe and hobnail prints. The party broke up at the village centre, Oldfield leaving for his headquarters, the constable turning in at his home and Littlejohn making for Briar Cottage.

The maid opened the door to the Inspector and conducted him to the drawing-room to wait the arrival of Wynyard. The place was stuffy and smelled of damp. Two heavy oil-paintings hung on the walls. An abundance of photographs in frames, scattered round the room. Albums, bound volumes of devotional magazines, novels of a moral type, a stereoscope with a pile of views to fit it, arranged in orderly fashion on tables of bamboo or of other Victorian styles. An old plush-upholstered suite, with a sofa; a heavy sideboard. Antimacassars on the suite; lace cushions on the sofa; a dish of artificial fruit and ugly vases containing paper flowers on the sideboard. A whatnot and an overmantel loaded with trifling ornaments, apparently souvenirs. Scores of them. Little salt-cellars, jugs, cups and saucers bearing coats-of-arms. Coloured tumblers, bone napkin rings and paper-knives with inscriptions concerning the resorts of their origin. A glass globe which, when shaken, caused a snowstorm over the house and church in its inside. Littlejohn was shaking the globe when the door opened and the Rev. Athelstan Wynyard entered. He was carrying Littlejohn's card in his hand. He gave the detective a flabby handshake.

"Inspector Littlejohn. Ah, yes. Pray be seated. Smoke, if you wish. My cousin never allowed smoking in here, but the smell of tobacco will do the place good."

Littlejohn expressed his condolences.

"Very sad. Indeed a tragedy, and you may rely on my co-operation, as far as is possible, in laying by the heels the monster responsible."

Wynyard was a tall, heavily-built man. Dark, sleek hair; tanned, almost baked skin; large, heavy face; brown eyes, with slightly bloodshot whites. Heavy lips which seemed to be prevented from sagging only by an effort of will. A well-preserved man for a missionary labouring in the South Seas. Evidently knew how to take care of himself and his stomach!

Mr. Wynyard was on his guard. Littlejohn felt he had something on his mind which was causing him uneasiness.

"I gather you're Miss Tither's nearest relative and as such you're probably in her confidence, sir. Now, in the course of our enquiries, we have learned that she wrote and posted a letter to you last Sunday and that she expected you to meet her at a roadside tea-house on the Evingdon Road on the morning she was murdered. Further, you did not keep the appointment. Can you explain the position?"

The clergyman looked sheepish and plucked his lower lip in embarrassment. Then, he hemmed and hawed guiltily. Littlejohn, his pipe burning nicely, his eyes mild and twinkling, waited in patience.

"Well... well... ahem... it's this way, Inspector. My cousin apparently has been under some misapprehension concerning my position with the missionary society I serve. She thought I was in some outpost, engaged on active evangelical work, whereas, I am the business agent for the society at the main port in our group of islands. Many of my colleagues are, of course, up country, but I remain at the port..."

Aha, thought the Inspector. Miss Tither thought you a hero and made you her heir on the strength of it! Somebody put her wise and she got mad. As though reading his thoughts, the minister continued.

"... The matter was never discussed between us, until someone must have vindictively spoken about my duties. My conscience is quite clear, my dear Inspector. I'm doing a very vital job, in spite of the fact that I say it myself, a very vital job, for which my employers think I have a flair. Were I not suited for it, I would be in the other parts of the vineyard, serving as missionary."

"You never told Miss Tither, then, just what your job was?"

"No. She wrote now and then and I answered her letters, giving the collective experiences and duties, rather than dwelling on my own small part."

In other words, he's passed himself off as a missionary to please the old girl and capture her imagination and money, thought the detective, and then added aloud: "Now about the letter, sir. Can you come to that?"

"It was strange in tone and content, Inspector. But first, let me say with emphasis, I was *not* in the vicinity at the time of the crime. My colleagues in London will fully confirm that state-ment. I was at our headquarters in Paternoster Row. When I stayed with my cousin—I was lecturing at Evingdon and other places at the time, raising funds for the Cause—I gave her an out-line of my proposed itinerary until I was due to sail back in the middle of next month. According to plan, I should have been in Leicester on Sunday, Monday and Tuesday of this week. Instead, I received a wire to return to headquarters for a conference first thing on Monday. I gave Miss Tither the address of my host-to-be in Leicester and said I would be pleased to hear from her there and, if she cared to make the journey, would welcome her visit whilst I was in the vicinity. She addressed her letter to me, care of Mr. Hawker, my host. It arrived on Monday, just after I'd left, and Hawker re-addressed it to me in London. It reached me too late for me to keep an appointment which she suggested for the morning of her death. I wired, but, alas, she was no more when the message reached this house."

The parson's face assumed a lugubrious expression. Littlejohn half expected Wynyard to strike up a homily on the transience of human existence or drone off into the burial service. Instead, he took a letter from his pocket. He hesitated and then, opening it, read it to his listener in an unctuous, resonant voice, reminiscent of the lectern.

"Miss Tither's letter goes:

'DEAR ATHELSTAN,

Information of a rather distressing kind has been com-municated to me this week-end. I hope it is libellous, in which case, I shall know what to do. I must tell you that a certain Mr. Lorrimer of this village, who has connections in your field of labour in the South Seas, tells me that your work consists, not of converting the heathen to The Light, but of acting as what he calls shipping-agent for the Society you serve.

I cannot understand this, in view of what you have given me to understand and the anecdotes concerning how you have saved so many souls from destruction, which you have related to me. I would like to see you at once. I have meditated and prayed on this matter and at last made up my mind what procedure to adopt. I would like you to come here to discuss things, but, until you have vindicated yourself, I feel embarrassment will be saved to both of us if we meet outside. A friend of mine, Miss Satchell, keeps a roadside café on the Evingdon Road, at the junction of the Stretton Road and I suggest you meet me there at 10.45 on Wednesday of this week. There is a good train—the only express of the day—which leaves Leicester at 8.15, arriving in Evingdon at 9.45. You will have ample time to get to Miss Satchell's by a quarter to eleven. I would like you to bring some clearer evidence of your activities and duties, if you please.

You will appreciate, Athelstan, that should the story which I am told prove correct, I shall have to alter my Will. I was leaving you my small worldly wealth for the expansion of the Kingdom through your work and should this not be practicable, in view of your more restricted duties—and, may I say, the fact that you have deceived me—I propose to replace your name by that of a charity in which I am deeply interested at home.

I pray that this statement I have heard may be false and
that you will be able to refute it. In such case, I propose
to take legal action against the slanderer. Otherwise, it
pains me to say that you and I have come to the parting
of the ways.

I have written frankly to you and not without pain and
prayer. I feel that you should know what is troubling my
mind beforehand in order that you may be prepared to
meet it. Should you clear the matter to my entire satisfaction, I will beg you on my knees to forgive me.

I am anxiously and hopefully awaiting our meeting.

Yours sincerely,

ETHEL TITHER.'"

Mr. Wynyard sheepishly raised his eyes from the letter as he ceased
reading and gazed at Littlejohn. It was obvious that Miss Tither's
suspicions were correct and that she had been accidentally or wilfully misled; probably the latter.

"I'd like a copy of that letter, Mr. Wynyard. Perhaps you'll lend
me the original until I can have one made? The contents will be
treated as confidentially as possible."

The missionary handed over the document and Littlejohn put
it in his notebook.

"And now, sir. About your movements at the time of the crime.
You were in London, you say."

"Yes, Inspector. I left Leicester the first thing Monday morning. I stayed at my usual hotel, 'The Peveril', in Coram Street, and
attended conferences at our headquarters in Paternoster Row. I
was there from ten until noon on Wednesday and the Secretary

of the Society will confirm that. The details are: Mr. Alexander Colquitt, Secretary, The Jabez Colquitt Mission, Colquitt House, Paternoster Row, London, E.C.4."

Littlejohn noted the particulars.

"I take it the funeral will be to-morrow, Mr. Wynyard."

"Yes, at 2 o'clock in the churchyard here."

"Thank you for your help, sir."

They parted and Littlejohn made his way to "The Bell", there to telephone to Cromwell, his subordinate at Scotland Yard, to check Wynyard's alibi. Here indeed was a motive for the crime, if Wynyard was about to be cut out of Miss Tither's Will. He was hardly the type to commit murder, however. More likely to rely on unctuous persuasion.

His business at the inn finished, the detective made his way through the village to Mr. Haxley's cottage. He thought a word with one of the last to see Miss Tither alive was called for, in addition to the fact that he wanted to check up on Harriwinckle's earlier impressions.

Mr. Haxley was at home and the Inspector was ushered into his study, where the stocky little man was improving the binding of what appeared to be second-hand books, by pasting strips of thin leather inside the backs.

"Glad to see you, Inspector," greeted the infidel, the object of so much tractarian bombardment by Miss Tither. Anyone more unlike a heathen could not be imagined.

"Excuse me carrying on with this job. We can talk as we work, eh? These are some volumes of *Cruden's Concordance* I picked up for a song in Evingdon the other day. I'm just putting them ship-shape and then I'll give 'em to Claplady. Not got much room for this kind of stuff myself, but it's a public duty to see that every parson has a *Cruden*. Old Claplady hasn't, so I'm giving him one. Help yourself to a cigar, Inspector. Those in the box there are good ones. Put a few in your pocket."

This perfect spate of goodwill almost bewildered Littlejohn. He accepted a cigar, but declined to carry any off with him.

"I called about your last meeting with Miss Tither, Mr. Haxley. We know now that she eventually arrived at Satchell's tea-rooms after leaving you, but I wonder if you saw anyone about, in the field or on the road, after she left you."

"Not a soul, Inspector, except the little girl carrying the beer to the harvesters. By the way, will you have a drink? I'm just going to have one myself."

Without waiting for an answer, Haxley rang the bell and told his manservant to bring in a couple of bottles of lager beer. Having drunk each other's health, the two men resumed their conversation.

"Can you give me any information concerning what was particularly agitating Miss Tither on the fatal morning? Mr. Claplady says he saw her in earnest discussion with you for quite a time. Could you tell me the topic? Perhaps something said, however trifling, might throw light on the case."

"The main topic was *me!*" said Haxley, removing his cigar and emitting, with a volume of smoke, a burst of loud, resonant laughter. He looked over the top of his glasses at Littlejohn.

"You see, I'm an agnostic and Miss Tither would persist in trying to make me otherwise, by bombarding me with tracts and arguments. I couldn't stand the woman, myself. Too sure of her own place in the Kingdom and always touting for new members.

As you know, I met her on her way to the Evingdon Road as I was out shooting in the glebe meadow. She stopped me with a tale about Voltaire; one I'd heard a hundred times before about his death-bed horrors and repentance. All bunkum and historically incorrect, and I told her so. She gave me a tract about the way of the ungodly perishing as she left me."

"Did she say anything about finding one of her tracts with a rude word written across it?"

"No. What was the word?"

Littlejohn told him. "Pah, not a bit funny, Inspector, is it? A poor sort of argument, mud-slinging. She wasn't quite as ardent as usual that morning, however. She'd other things on her mind."

"In what way?"

"She was bothering her head about certain charitable institutions. Why ask me, I don't know. Probably thought that having been in business in London, I knew everything about everybody there."

"What charities did she refer to?"

"The Home Gospel Society, or something, was one. The other was the Jabez Colquitt Mission. I'd never heard of the first; the second I knew a bit about. She talked of instituting enquiries about the Home Gospel. Going to leave some money to it, she said. And she was a bit mysterious about the Colquitt Mission. I told her what I knew about it."

"And what was that, Mr. Haxley, if you don't mind?"

Haxley laid aside his gum brush and books and drew up a chair. "It's rather a long tale and probably quite irrelevant to your case, but I'll be as brief as I can."

He crossed his legs, took a drink of his beer.

"I know quite a lot about the Colquitt Mission. You see, I was at school in Selchester with a fellow who runs a rival show. Percy Prettypenny he was called. I remember most of the congregation of the chapel we both attended kowtowing to Percy's father and mother, who had great possessions made in penny-bazaars. I can almost hear Old Prettypenny publicly praying to the Chairman of the Kingdom of Heaven, in which he and his wife were large share-holders, for blessings on 'our brethren of Inja, China, Sahmoa, and the ahlands of the sea'. I can see in my mind's eye, too, Mr. Prettypenny and Percy, one a twenty-five-years-younger replica of the other and both with bowler hats a size too small for them."

Littlejohn wondered where all this rigmarole was leading. The old chap seemed lonely and wanted a long talk apparently. The detective settled down to bear it a little longer in the hope of gleaning a few scraps of useful information.

"... Well, Percy fell in love with Miss Bose, a native mission-ary on leave from India. A coloured lady, if you please! Never! screamed Mrs. Prettypenny in a fiery interview between Miss Bose and the three Prettypennies—or Pretty-pence, whichever you like. Haw! Haw! Percy pointed out his belief in the brother-hood of man and the fatherhood of God over coloured ladies and white gentlemen. Envisaging half-caste heirs to a penny-bazaar fortune, Mrs. P. remained firm and her husband remained silent. Miss Bose, I understand, politely informed Mrs. Prettypenny that her Indian ancestors were civilized and distinguished in arts and science whilst those of Mrs. P. were chasing each other with stone clubs round the Weald of Kent, and then eloped with Percy to the Islands of the Seas, where they converted many heathen and were full of good works. Percy must have taken a fancy to me, for he kept up a correspondence with me and I still hear from him about twice a year."

"But does this affect the Colquitt Mission, in any way?" interposed Littlejohn. "That's what I'm anxious to know."

"Oh, yes. But the whole tale's damn funny. Have another cigar and put one or two in your pocket. They're good ones.

"I'll try to be brief, then. Pandalu is an island, the largest of the group of about twenty, in the South Seas. These are served by two missions, the Jabez Colquitt and the Samuel Corkish-Aspinwall Crusaders. Both Colquitt and Sam Corkish (took on the Aspinwall for swank!) were traders there in the early days and, after making fortunes in persuading natives to dive for pearls for pittances, they founded rival societies to propitiate the gods and convert their former workmen from happy, free-and-easy heathenism to sin-tormented worship of a jealous and terrible god. They'd have been better amalgamated, but the Samuelites differed from the Jabezites by contending that sprinkling by water as the key to the kingdom of heaven was a lazy, effete and insufficient way of opening the door of grace. *Baptizo*, means I DIP and *not* I SPRINKLE, in the holy writ, was an evergreen argument of the Crusaders and nothing short of total immersion would do for them. As bathing in the limpid pools of the islands was a speciality of the natives there, the Crusaders had and have the greater following."

Littlejohn shuffled in his chair. This theological splitting of hairs was all right for someone with plenty of time, but to a busy man it was torture.

"That chair uncomfortable? Try the armchair, Inspector. Well, this is what I'm getting at. Young Percy Prettypenny is the head of the Corkishers; Wynyard is Reverend Shipping Superintendent of the Colquittites. Athelstan is Percy's pet aversion and never a letter comes without something about him. Wynyard orders supplies from England and Australia, sees they arrive on the monthly boat, engages labour to unload them and ship them up country or to the other posts, attends to the mails and greets newcomers, as well as paying 'em and bidding 'em god-speed when they go on leave. In his case, according to Percy, the white-man's burden is not heavy, for he has an efficient native clerk, who deputizes for him on all except ceremonial occasions, at a wage worth about two and eightpence a week. This allows him to spend his ample leisure dozing beneath the shade of his gourd or on his veranda, assisted by long drinks of lime-juice—or something else when nobody's looking—and an electric fan. In other words Wynyard is just a clerical bag of bluff, unctuous, urbane and self-seeking. But the funny part of it is, he gets away with it. So much so, that there's some talk of making him suffragan bishop of the Islands of the Seas. Over here in England, one hears of his lecturing to crowded audiences on the wonderful works he's performing in the far-flung field of service and the hardships he undergoes parading among his scattered flock."

"Did you tell that to Miss Tither when she met you?"

"Yes. Perhaps not in so many words, but I told her that I had it on the highest authority, from a reliable source, that he was just a humbug and if she cared to see some of Prettypenny's letters, I'd show 'em to her. I'm not religious myself, and I don't meddle with other folks' honest beliefs, but I do draw the line at bunkum and bluff. But, mind you, I wasn't the first to arouse her suspicions and disillusion her. Somebody else, she didn't say who, had been at her."

"That's very useful and I'm much obliged to you. Well, I think I'll be getting on with the job. Thanks for the hospitality, Mr. Haxley. I'll let you get on with your bookbinding, sir."

"Don't you want to hear the rest of the tale, then?"

"Eh?"

"Well, Old Prettypenny, left at home, his wife dead and his penny-bazaars converted into a limited company of sixpenny stores, began to pine for his lost boy, so he packed his bag and sailed for Pandalu. His arrival there created a commotion, I'll tell you. Old Ephraim Prettypenny, clad in his ceremonial top-hat and frock coat and with his long white beard, was mistaken, when he disembarked, for the god of battles himself, and nothing he or his seed could do would convince the natives otherwise. Hundreds saw the light and were dipped. When, at length, the old chap died, worn out by the attentions of his worshippers, he was found to have forgotten to alter his Will and to have left all his money to Salem Chapel, Selchester, greatly to the satisfaction of the elders there, who straightway began to quarrel among themselves concerning ways of spending it. Meanwhile, the surviving prophets of the great god Prettypenny, now interred on a mountain-top in a magnificent mausoleum, together with the mechanical contraption for the conquest of deafness, worn on his chest during life and regarded by the natives as big medicine, lived happy ever after on reflected glory."

Littlejohn slipped away whilst Mr. Haxley was still lost in convulsions of mirth at the tale.

He almost felt sorry for Miss Tither and her fruitless efforts to make this jovial old sinner forsake his ways.

In turning in the direction of the house of Mr. Lorrimer, the next name on his agenda, Littlejohn hoped that he was not jumping out of the frying-pan into the fire and finding another garrulous eccentric. As he strolled through the centre of the village on his way to Holly Bank, the detective had to run the gauntlet of knots of idlers and gossiping women at cottage doors. Judging from the odour hanging round "The Bell", Littlejohn's dinner was in the oven. Hens scratched in the ditches, cats sunned themselves, dogs snuffed about the roadside. Somewhere, some-one was rattling milk churns and in the distance the clatter of a reaping-machine could be heard. The clank of the anvil and the softer blows of the hammers on hot metal sounded from the smithy. A dog-cart of ancient design jogged along to Hilary Parva and on the main Evingdon road, by way of contrast, the snarling exhaust of a sports-car roared and died away. Two clipped bushes of holly marked Littlejohn's destination. He knocked his pipe on the gate post until the dottle fell out, and turned in.

CHAPTER IX

The Bag of Bluff

CONCEALED BEHIND A THICK HEDGE OF PRIVET, MOUNTED atop a roughcast wall, Holly Bank reveals little of itself to passers-by, but once past the gate, Littlejohn was surprised at the primness of the place. The garden was a model of neatness and order. Although the countryside was showing signs of autumn, there was not a stray leaf on the paths, all the dead flowers had been removed and the bedding plants still seemed in their prime. Late roses flourished, large clumps of Michaelmas daisies made masses of colour, and in beds set in the lawns, geraniums sprouted pink and scarlet. The grass was well rolled and finely cut and resembled a costly, even carpet.

The house itself was as orderly as the grounds. Its paintwork was prim and clean, its stuccoed walls freshly creamwashed and its green shutters trim and business-like. The place resembled the villa of a well-to-do Frenchman of the Midi. A neat, good-looking young maid took Littlejohn's card and asked him to wait in the drawing-room. The place was light and airy and furnished in good taste. A thick green carpet yielded luxuriously beneath the feet. The furniture was well made, costly and comfortable. On the walls a few pleasing etchings and over the fireplace a picture which Littlejohn greatly admired. It was a genuine Corot, although the detective could not be sure about it.

Mr. Lorrimer joined his visitor almost at once. A middle-sized, dapper man in a well-made suit of dark tweed, with a fresh, clean-shaven face, tight, thin lips, prominent, pointed nose and a large, bald, dome-shaped head surrounded by a fringe of thin brown hair. Deep-set grey eyes, slightly bulging, behind rimless spectacles, with thin, straw-coloured eyebrows. Fastidiousness, neatness, cleanliness, seemed the prominent features of his make-up. Littlejohn particularly noticed the man's hands, which were rather large, but scrupulously well kept. The handshake Mr. Lorrimer gave the detective was strong and firm and reminded Littlejohn that the vicar had mentioned that the tenant of Holly Bank was a well-known local pianist, who practised several hours a day for his own amusement and never gave any public exhibition of his talent.

Lorrimer waved his visitor to a chair.

"Now, Inspector. I suppose you have called to see me about something or other in connection with this horrible murder business. I don't know how I can assist, but I am willing to co-operate, of course. Fire away."

"It's just one point I wanted your help about, Mr. Lorrimer. Miss Tither's maid tells me that, after church last Sunday, you gave Miss Tither some information which greatly distressed her and as her almost immediate reaction when she reached home, was to write to her cousin, Mr. Wynyard, and arrange a rendez-vous to discuss his work in the missionary field, I wonder if it concerned him."

"Yes, it did, Inspector. I simply told Miss Tither something I'd heard concerning her relative and his goings-on. You see, he's been lecturing about the place lately—gave a well-attended address at Evingdon, for example—and leading people to believe he's a perfect Apostle Paul of the South Seas, whereas, I believe, he's nothing more or less than a commercial agent, or something."

"How did you come across this news?"

"Unfortunately for Mr. Wynyard, a friend of mine, once the cashier of a London bank, now the manager of the agency of the English and Australian South Sea Bank in Pandalu, happened to be in Evingdon at the time of the lectures and attended one. Judge his surprise when Mr. Wynyard, whom he knows well, got on his hind legs and told what amounted to a rattling yarn, but with no basis in fact. Mossley, that's my friend, had to choose between leaving the place at once or denouncing old Wynyard as a fake. He chose the former alternative, being a rather shy man. He was glad he'd done so later, for he's one with a sense of humour and enjoyed a good laugh about it when he'd cooled down. I happened to fall across him in Evingdon one day and he told me about it, in passing."

"Did you make a special point of telling Miss Tither about it?"

"Oh no. We were just passing the time of day as we walked to the road after church and she mentioned Wynyard having gone on another lecture tour in another district. Before I knew what I was saying almost, I'd blurted out Mossley's tale. She was on it in a minute and showed signs of great distress. She insisted on walking home with me and hearing a full account of it. I tried to cry it down when I saw how hard she was taking it. It seems, that on the strength of Wynyard's work, she'd left him quite a lot of money in her Will, for the express purpose, she said, of encouraging what he's told her was his life-work. When I left her, she was very agitated, I'll tell you."

Littlejohn looked Lorrimer in the eyes, but an ingenuous gaze met his own. Somehow, however guilty Wynyard might have been, it seemed a wretched trick to make a point of sneaking on him.

"There's nothing more you can tell me which might help us in the case, Mr. Lorrimer?"

"I'm afraid not. You see, I knew very little of Miss Tither or her activities. To be quite candid, I gave her a very wide berth. I'd heard something of her goings-on in the way of scandalmongering and, shall we say, social work in the village and the less I had to do with her, the better I felt it would be for me."

Lorrimer bared a mouthful of even, white false teeth in a grin and gave Littlejohn a knowing nod.

"Just as a matter of routine, sir, could you tell me what you were doing on the morning of the crime?"

Lorrimer raised his thin eyebrows.

"Am I among the list of suspects, then? I'm sure I can't see why, knowing little of the lady and caring less about her. However, I can't give you a cast-iron alibi. All I can say is, I was playing the piano from ten-thirty until about noon. I usually do. A friend of mine happened to have sent me a new sonata he'd written and it reached me by first post on Wednesday. I set about it and played it through twice. Not much of an alibi, I'll grant you, but the maids would hear me playing. There's the piano."

Lorrimer indicated a grand piano, standing near the window, with manuscript music lying carelessly on the top of it. Before Littlejohn could speak, he had rung the bell.

"You'd better check that with the servants, for what it's worth. They were both in at the time. You ask 'em; I'll not spoil it by putting a leading question."

The Inspector felt nettled at Lorrimer's fussiness. He preferred to work in his own way. The maid who had opened the door to him earlier appeared. Lorrimer languidly waved his hand as if passing on the girl to the detective.

"The Inspector has a question or two to ask you and Alice. Send her in when he's finished with you."

"I'm just wanting to confirm that you heard your master playing the piano on Wednesday last, from about ten-thirty until noon. Can you remember?"

"Well, he plays most mornings, sir. Now let me see, Wednesday." The girl struck a pose suggestive of deep thought. "Oh yes, it was Wednesday you said you'd have your morning coffee half an hour earlier, wasn't it, sir? And when I brought it, you said you didn't want disturbing, as you'd something special you'd be working on."

Lorrimer beamed at the girl, baring his teeth again.

"That's it, Grace."

"And you played without stopping for nearly an hour, then went on again till twelve."

"How do you know the times, Grace?" asked Littlejohn.

"Well, I knew when the master started, because of his havin' his coffee at hal'-past ten instead of eleven. And I remember him stopping just after I'd looked at the kitchen clock on account of layin' for lunch."

The girl seemed settled for a thoroughgoing palaver, but Littlejohn was satisfied and dismissed her with thanks, asking her to send Alice in and not tell her what it was about.

Alice was plump and shy, a country girl in contrast to her senior, Grace, who bore evidence of town training. She blushed and stammered. Yes, she'd heard the piano playing. It only stopped once for a minute or two and then went on. As far as she could say, it started just after she'd made the master's coffee and sent it in. Early it was. Yes, about a half before eleven. The playing stopped about twelve. She knew because Grace showed her the clock and told her to get a move on with the potatoes. Then, Mr. Lorrimer rang for her just after he stopped playing to tell her something about some ink he'd upset on the carpet. She mopped it up; you could see the mark faintly still just by the piano. Littlejohn thanked and dismissed her and she almost ran from the room, full of relief and anxiety to compare notes with Grace.

"Did you see Miss Tither again after your morning meeting, Mr. Lorrimer?"

"Yes, strangely enough, I did. I happened to have nothing much to do in the evening, so I went to church again. A rather unusual thing for me. I was on my way home when Miss Tither overtook me and told me she'd written to her cousin, asking him to meet her on Wednesday and that she then proposed to give him a chance of denying the story. I was rather dumfounded, I'll tell you. I never thought for a moment that what I'd meant to be a casual comment, would develop into something so serious. I told her so, too."

"And what did she say?"

"She thanked me rather profusely. Said that if what I said was true, I'd prevented her making a great mistake. Otherwise, she would be very annoyed with whoever had started the scandal. That is, if Wynyard vindicated himself, I presume. Anyway, it hadn't anything to do with me, so I didn't bother about it again. We parted at the village centre and I went on home. I do feel pleased, however, that I put her wise to the way in which that bag of bluff, her cousin, had taken her in."

"Bag of bluff? I seem to have heard that expression before to-day."

"Probably from Old Haxley. It's his epithet. I met him this morning and it seems he's heard a similar tale from another source. Funny, the pair of us in the same village should have struck the same tale of distant goings-on from separate sources."

Mr. Lorrimer had a habit of crisply finishing off his sentences, as though biting into a stream of verbiage to terminate its flow. As he enlarged on the piece of scandal he shared with Haxley, he smacked his lips as he chewed the phrases, as though thoroughly enjoying its savour.

Littlejohn thanked him and bade him good day. Remembering the funeral of Miss Tither, which was to take place at two o'clock, the detective hastened his steps in the direction of his lunch. He would join the outer circle of sympathizers, he decided. He might capture some impression from the gathering and have the chance of sizing-up the mourners. Besides, the lawyer from Evingdon was arriving and, later, would, as arranged with Oldfield, read the Will and then go through Miss Tither's private papers with the police in attendance.

As he crossed the road, Littlejohn heard pattering feet behind him. It was Mr. Claplady, hurrying home to his own lunch and kicking his cassock about with each step. He waved to Littlejohn and hurried towards him.

"Hullo, Inspector. I hope you'll be at the graveside this afternoon. It will be symbolic, I think, don't you? A sign, shall we say, that justice is working for the poor lady. See you later, then.

Good-bye, good-bye." The cassock began to flap again, but suddenly the vicar turned in his tracks and confidentially addressed Littlejohn once more. "Things never happen singly, do they, Inspector? Do you know, I've just had a visit from Polly Druce. She and young Elliman, one of the grooms at the Hall, and now serving with the Forces, are being married to-morrow by special license and want me to perform the ceremony. Most unexpected! Surprising, I'm sure! He's got twenty-four hours' leave and they've suddenly made up their minds. I'd no idea there was anything between them... Well, till we meet again..." The feet tittupped away and the vicar turned the corner, still muttering to himself with surprise.

"Well, well," said Littlejohn to himself with a chuckle and he followed his nose in the direction of what he was sure was roast beef and Yorkshire pudding.

CHAPTER X

The Will

I T BEGAN TO RAIN AT LUNCH-TIME AND AT THE APPOINTED
hour of Miss Tither's funeral, a steady downpour had set in.
Littlejohn stood in the doorway of "The Bell" in company with the
landlord, his wife and a knot of regulars and watched the hearse,
drawn by two steaming horses, pass the place at a speed which
combined maximum haste with maximum respect. Three cars
followed, their occupants invisible through the steamed windows.
Littlejohn put on his raincoat and made his way to the churchyard
at a discreet distance. The weather had not kept indoors those
who regarded a funeral as a special treat and a motley crowd of
sightseers and sympathizers formed a ragged procession behind
the cortège. Umbrellas bobbed and the footfalls of the walkers
rang on the road. There was no sound of voices; only the patter
of feet, the drone of cars in low funereal gear, the clip, clop of
the horses, the hiss and patter of the rain. At the church, another
contingent of uninvited mourners and spectators waited, shelter-
ing under the lych-gate and in the porch. A few hardy ones hung
about under the dripping trees. They greeted each other with
solemn nods, unspeaking, or just whispering, and settled down
grimly to wait for the graveside ceremony. Littlejohn entered the
graveyard by a side gate and took his stand under a chestnut tree
which dropped capsules of rain down his neck and caused him
to button up his mackintosh and drag his hat down over his ears.

Mr. Claplady emerged from the church at length, a choirboy holding a large umbrella over his head. He was followed by Mr. Brassey, the lawyer, Wynyard and two decayed-looking ladies in faded black, presumably relatives many times removed claiming their graveside rights. Sarah Russell was there, accompanied by Thornbush. Both were in new black clothes and carried umbrellas, which were ineffective against the downpour which seemed slowly to be converting the cloth of their garments into satin. Thornbush wore a superior religious expression, as though full to the brim with knowledge of death and the grave and how to deprive them of their sting and victory. He looked ready at any moment to brush aside the vicar and himself commit the victim in a burst of psalms. Mr. Claplady droned like a hive of his own bees. There was a smell of earth, mould, dead leaves and woodsmoke. Shuffling and sliding on the mound of upthrown earth, the sexton and his mate carried the coffin and poised it over the grave. Mr. Claplady mumbled on and the burden was lowered. Clay and stones rattled on the lid of the coffin, one by one the mourners gave a last peep into the depths, and then the official procession disintegrated and there was a rush back to the waiting cars. The sexton arranged the wreaths of sodden flowers by the side of the path and stood waiting with his underling. It was the sign that the public were admitted. Women surged over the grass, read the tickets on the wreaths, chattered to each other, peered down at the coffin, flung handfuls of mud and stones on it with a show of respect, and melted away, complaining to their neighbours that they were getting their death of cold. When all the bedraggled crew had melted away, a small, straight-backed woman dressed in an ancient raincoat with leg-of-mutton sleeves, hurried to the graveside, her umbrella aloft like a banner, her stride purposeful, her lips a thin line. She did not hesitate, but walked straight to the hole, took up a handful of the muddy earth and stones and flung them on the coffin with a gesture of spiteful determination and vindictiveness. Then she marched away.

The two labourers were hastily shovelling-in the earth. Littlejohn approached them.

"Who was that?" he asked.

"Ar?" said the sexton, a drop on the end of his nose and rain on his whiskers like small icicles.

"Who was the woman who just left?"

"Ar... that be Mrs. Weekes o' Upper Hilary Farm, that be. Praper caution she be... Naw then, Ishmael, carn't ye shovel farster. Oi be chilled to the marrer."

Oldfield appeared, clad in oilskins and sou'wester. Littlejohn was glad to see his cheery, red face after what had just passed. He was puffing a large calabash. They greeted each other cordially.

"How's it going, Littlejohn?"

"Oh, so-so. Not taking shape yet. I'll tell you about it in a drier spot than this and with something warm inside us."

"I've seen Brassey. They'll probably be clear of mourners in an hour or so. We're to meet at five at Briar Cottage. He won't touch letters or papers until we arrive."

"Good. Then I suggest that we see what they have to cheer and warm us at 'The Bell' and I can tell you how things are going."

Without more ado they set their course for the pub and left the principal character of their strange case to rest in peace under the dripping trees.

★

At Briar Cottage, Sarah Russell answered the door in response to their knock. She had been weeping and her face was swollen and her eyes red-rimmed. Mr. Brassey was in a state of great excitement when the Inspectors entered the drawing-room. Wynyard was seated in an armchair by the hearth in an attitude of broken despair. The lawyer turned a furious face on his visitors.

"The arrival of the police is all that's required to complete the prettiest bit of damned tomfoolery I've seen for many a day. I wish, gentlemen, you were calling to take off into custody that silly Sarah Russell and her psalm-prating Thornbush."

The two detectives, surprised at their reception, gazed questioningly at Mr. Brassey. His pale face was suffused with rage, his thin hands flew hither and thither furiously gesticulating, his toupet-like hair was deranged. He looked more than ever like a bellicose sparrow emerging from a ding-dong battle with rivals for bread-crumbs.

"Good afternoon, gentlemen," moaned Wynyard, raising a flushed face. His lips were dry and he was perspiring to his very eyes.

"As if we hadn't enough on our hands without this further complication," chattered Brassey, his false teeth clicking. "We've just discovered that the Will I outlined to you the other day in my office is *not* the last Will and Testament of my late client, but has been set aside by a later document, drawn up in Miss Tither's own hand on Monday last, witnessed by Sarah Russell and that confounded Thornbush and not disclosed until an hour ago!"

Oldfield passed his hand across his hair in puzzlement and Littlejohn whistled softly.

"You may well whistle. I never heard such damned nonsense in my life. In a revulsion of feeling against Mr. Wynyard here…"

At this there was a groan from the offended party.

"... Miss Tither decided to alter her Will. Instead of consulting me, as she ought to have done, she carefully copied her duplicate of the document I held, but changed the bequests. The new Will is as before, with the exception that Wynyard here is cut out altogether and" (more groans from the corner) "... and... the residue is left to the Home Gospel Alliance, if you please."

"But what have I done, thus to be treated, slighted, humiliated?" moaned Wynyard, addressing the room in general.

"But surely, Mr. Brassey," interjected Littlejohn, "you ought to have been made aware of this change, if not before, then immediately after the death of Miss Tither. If Russell knew of it, she ought to have told you."

"That's what makes me so furious. If I'd the power to do it, that girl and her pious humbug of a follower wouldn't get a penny. It seems that Miss Tither drew up this new—and by the way, perfectly legal—document, signed it and had it witnessed. Then, she locked it in the drawer of that bureau. She told Russell in the presence of Thornbush, that the new Will was an emergency one. She'd found out something concerning Wynyard and wished to protect herself in case it were true. If the story were untrue, she would destroy the homemade document; otherwise, it would stand, and if meanwhile 'swift death o'ertook her' (the words of that canting humbug!), Russell was to hand the new Will to me."

"And why wasn't it done at once?" questioned Oldfield.

"Thornbush! He had the impertinence to tell the girl to refrain until after the funeral. That was the time for Wills, he said, damn him! So the pair of them sat on it until I produced my document and then sprang their mine."

"But aren't the circumstances under which the Will was executed sufficient to invalidate it?" asked Littlejohn.

"I shall fight! I shall fight!" screeched Wynyard, suddenly exhibiting spirit.

"It won't do you a ha'porth of good. This is a perfectly legal document and there are at least half-a-dozen people who will swear that she was in her right mind at the time of executing it. I'm sorry for you, Wynyard, very sorry. But what I'm furious about, is the manner of its being done and the behaviour of that pair of fools. I've given Sarah a piece of my mind and I've packed off Thornbush with a flea in his ear. He's not to come near this place until after probate, or I'll have him pitched out on his neck. And now, gentlemen, I propose we cool down and go through Miss Tither's private papers. I'm sorry, Wynyard, very sorry, but you've no standing here now. I suggest you retire to your room and rest a bit to recover from the shock. You'll get over it."

The lawyer exhibited his human side, put his arm through that of the distressed missionary and led him to the door.

"Now, gentlemen, to business. Let's see what we have in this desk."

The receptacle for Miss Tither's private papers was a large bureau of ancient design, standing in one corner of the room. Brassey took a key from his pocket and opened the top drawer. "I hope we don't find any more damned Wills here," he said. "There's been enough bother as it is. I've had to send the Misses Golightly, distant cousins of the deceased, whom she seemed to have forgotten, I've had to send 'em home in a cab! Not even their fares for attending the funeral left to 'em!"

The top drawer of the desk contained a jumbled assembly of lumber. Last season's Christmas cards, tied in a neat bundle with the addresses of the senders pencilled on them in Miss Tither's hand. Evidently the cues for the greetings she intended to send next time. Stationery, envelopes, sealing-wax, labels, pens, nibs and account-books. A pile of old passbooks and cheque-book stubs. The three men turned over the miscellaneous articles and the policemen laid aside the account-books and cheque counterfoils for later consideration. The next drawer held a current cheque-book and passbook which were placed with the old ones for closer scrutiny. Piles of old bills, circulars, letters. The latter mainly from relatives, including Mr. Wynyard. Then, came a stack of business correspondence, clipped by a large paper-fastener in one corner. Begging letters from individuals or charities, each neatly marked, "No", or "Leave", or again "Sent £5" or whatever the amount, with the date. Lastly, another batch of letters, similarly clipped. These were the most interesting find of all. They were all written from 11 Ropewalker Street, E.C.4, on paper headed "The Home Gospel Alliance for Bringing Sinners to Repentance". They were in date order and presented a brief history of Miss Tither's connection with that charity. She had apparently been a patron for about three years and remitted substantial sums from time to time. This file was placed with the accounts for comparison.

The bottom drawer was opened and found to contain tracts of all kinds, but the "improving" literature had strange bedfellows. About two dozen novels, in paper backs or cheap board, and usually bought by post or furtively from small shops. French, German, American, British works, all in English, of course. Some of them well known; others less common, but equally salacious. The three men looked at each other and smiled wryly. Mr. Brassey closed and locked the drawer. *"De mortuis…"* he muttered. "We'd better arrange for those to be quietly burned. Perhaps she bought them the better to understand the souls for which she thought she was working. Give her the benefit of the doubt."

They turned their attention to the items they had set aside. There was no doubt about it that Miss Tither's favourite charity was the Home Alliance. The correspondence, together with the passbooks, told the story plainly. The dead woman had been cunningly flattered and skilfully persuaded to support the efforts of the association, whatever these might have been. First came a leaflet, explaining the work of the body among the fallen of the slums and even the West End. Miss Tither, apparently interested, had sent five pounds, which brought an immediate and profuse reply, plus more literature. There was a pause, then another begging letter. This elicited ten pounds. The latter sum was evidently employed, or said to be employed, in setting an erring sister, specifically mentioned by name, on the right track. A week later, followed a letter from the erring one to the association expressing lifelong thanks and gratitude to the unknown benefactor, who had shown her the error of her ways. From then on, Miss Tither had become easy prey. Letter after letter followed. Cheques for £50 a time; flowery acknowledgments; copies of letters from those who had benefited. Then, about twelve months before her death, came the final honour. Miss Tither was made honorary vice-president of the society and her name appeared on the letter paper!

Brassey turned over the letters one by one and passed them to his companions. Littlejohn and Oldfield took out amounts on a piece of paper, and finally made an approximate total of sums paid to the Home Alliance by Miss Tither during her connection with it. In three years she had sent two thousand five hundred pounds! Now, she had left them the bulk of her estate! The three men were aghast.

"This isn't the first case I've come across," commented Brassey. "Flattery and the like often drive lonely folk such as Miss Tither crazy, or give 'em a blind spot. She fancied she was adopting all the sinning women in London and whoever's running this racket knew how to tackle her."

"By the way, have you ever heard of this charity before?" asked Littlejohn. "It's funny Miss Tither never seems to have properly investigated it."

Brassey turned over a pile of printed papers.

"You see, here they issue a proper balance sheet, duly audited by a firm of warranted accountants, showing income and expenditure. The show seems to be run properly. All these letters are signed by the paid secretary, Alcimas Mortimore, but the president seems to be the Rev. Peter Scarisdale, D.D., whoever he may be."

The lawyer pointed to two further letters which he had been scrutinizing.

"Miss Tither's evidently tried to arrange a personal interview with the D.D. See, here's his reply."

There followed an unctuous screed, explaining how busy the reverend gentleman was, and how his labours in the vineyard kept him fully employed. He would, however, be delighted to meet the generous benefactress at the first opportunity and would write her at an early date. Then came another letter of apology from Dr. Scarisdale. This time he was in Scotland and unable to meet Miss Tither in London, as suggested. Furthermore, he would not recommend visits by the lady to the various East-end vineyards of the Society. They were hardly the place for her. He was arranging for Mr. Mortimore to call on her at Hilary, however, and tell her in person of the work carried on, its fruits, and how her generous support was furthering it.

Mortimore evidently had paid a visit to Briar Cottage, for his letter of thanks for hospitality was filed; also a further note from him dated a few days later, expressing gratitude to Miss Tither for the promise of a legacy.

"There's something fishy about this business," said Brassey. "The way the poor lady seems to have been led up the garden path, but never allowed to see a thing, apparently kept from London and the field of activities, looks very funny to me. We'd better investigate it."

"You can leave that end to me, Mr. Brassey. Scotland Yard are already enquiring about the Home Gospel Alliance and this will include Mortimore, Scarisdale and Co. This looks to me like as pretty a piece of confidence trickery as I've seen for many a day."

They left the lawyer tidying the contents of the desk, but the detectives themselves took the accounts concerning the charity. "Let me know if I can help further," said Brassey. "I hold no brief for Wynyard. Tell you the truth, can't stand the fellow. But I hope you'll be able to put the cat among the pigeons in Ropewalker Street and make that legacy null and void by clapping the would-be beneficiaries under lock and key. Then the *status quo* having been restored, Wynyard will be able to retire from the South Seas. See you later, gentlemen."

Sarah Russell opened the door to the two detectives. Littlejohn paused on the step as she stood there, still red-eyed and nervous.

"Tell me, Sarah, why did Miss Tither call the new Will an emergency one? Now don't start weeping again. I'm not blaming you for what you've done; it's no business of mine. But it seems strange to me that Miss Tither should be in such a hurry to make a new Will before meeting Mr. Wynyard."

The maid sniffed loudly and her face grew resentful.

"I was a-goin' to tell Mr. Brassey about it, but 'e fell in sich a temper and wouldn't let me speak. Now, perhaps I can finish my story. Miss Tither said to me, confidential like—she not often telling me her private affairs, but this time seemin' so upset as to want somebody to confide in. Well, she tells me, 'Sarah,' she says, 'Sarah, I bin hearin' things about a relative of mine from Mr. Lorrimer, a man I greatly trust and respec' and who's prepared to prove them. I'm alterin' my Will at once, not in respec' of your share o' course, Sarah,' she sez, 'but in respec' of my relative's. Please bring in Mr. Thornbush, as I wants you to witness for me.' Well I brings in Walter and we signs and then Miss Tither sez to us both, 'I'm puttin' this in the drawer 'ere. If anything 'appens to me before I can see Mr. Brassey, you're to tell 'im it's 'ere. I'm meetin' my relative this week to ask what he's got to say for 'imself and if he can't satisfy me, then I'll 'ave the emergency Will drawn up proper by Mr. Brassey.'"

"But what's all this about emergency Wills? Surely, she didn't expect to die before Wednesday?"

"I don't know, sir. She seemed scared o' somethin'."

"Do you know what it was?"

"Well, somethin' 'appened when she was at Upper Hilary, gettin' the crabs from Mrs. Weekes. She came back without the crabs and very upset. 'Sarah,' says she, 'Mrs. Weekes is a funny woman and not nice at all. She's just told me I oughter be killed fer wot I've sed to 'er to-day, as if it wasn't the truth, and she oughter know it.' She seemed terribly put-out and perhaps that's why she made the emergency Will."

"Thank you, Sarah, that's very helpful. But why've you held all this back? Why didn't you tell me the other night?"

"Well, sir. It was Walter's advice to keep a still tongue and say as little as possible. Least said, soonest mended, says he, and that all this talk was like the cracklin' o' thorns beneath a pot. But after the way Mr. Brassey took on, I don't think Walter's advice is as good as I thought it was. In fact, sir, between you and me, I'm not decided whether to break it off with 'im. My confidence in 'im is shook. I've taken it to the Throne of Grace a time or two and now I'm waitin' for my answer."

"You think carefully about it, Sarah. Don't throw yourself and your money after the first man that comes."

"Oh, 'e ain't the first, by any means, sir!" said the maid and blushed.

"Well, good luck, Sarah, whatever you choose, only don't with-hold information from the police on anybody's advice in future."

At "The Bell" the detectives slaked their thirst after a dusty job and parted. Littlejohn telephoned to Detective-Sergeant Cromwell at Scotland Yard but found him absent on enquiries in the Tither case, but he had left a message confirming Wynyard's alibi. Then, he ordered his dinner for eight o'clock and set out for Upper Hilary Farm.

CHAPTER XI

The Horror at Upper Hilary

T HE RAIN HAD CEASED AND, AS LITTLEJOHN MADE HIS WAY through the village to the Evingdon cross-roads *en route* for Upper Hilary Farm, the wet highway glittered like a sheet of glass and the air was full of the smell of autumn leaves and damp grass. The sun was setting amid yellow-streaked clouds, boding no good for the morrow's weather. Parties of girls and women, with here and there a country lad or two, made their ways to the church, their arms loaded with evergreens, sheaves of wheat, cabbages, turnips and beetroots, or else carrying bags and baskets of apples, pears, or potatoes, for the following day was Harvest Home. Other villagers, clad in their better clothes, were standing about the village centre in knots, or ambling off to "The Bell" in search of convivial company. A small red 'bus pulled up at the Evingdon Cross and a stream of women and children, with a sprinkling of men in horsey attire, disembogued, laden with parcels of all shapes and sizes purchased at the weekly market at Evingdon. Saturday evening service was in full swing at the Methodist Chapel and, as Littlejohn turned right in search of the turning to Upper Hilary Farm, a loud burst of evangelical hymn-singing met him.

Yield not to temptation, for yielding is sin;
Each victory will help you some other to win...

Shrill women's piping, the tuneless rumble of a few basses. Above all, the wild soaring of a howling tenor, with a harmonium furiously bearing the whole along. The strength of the instrument waxed and waned in asthmatic pantings as the organist trod the pedals. Lights appeared one by one and curtains were drawn. Sarah Russell sat in the firelight of the kitchen at Briar Cottage, swaying to and fro happily in a rocking-chair. It was pleasant, she thought, to spend a little leisure away from the domination of Walter. She had made up her mind to put an end to it, then and there. There was a farmer at Fletney, beyond Evingdon, who winked invitingly as he passed Briar Cottage in his dog-cart. He was a widower, who had no call to make the long journey through Hilary on his way to Stretton Harcourt... From the open window of Holly Bank, a sparkling cascade of notes emerged, as Mr. Lorrimer played the last movement of Grieg's Piano Concerto, with an orchestral accompaniment on the radiogram.

In the kitchen at Upper Hilary Farm, the lamp had been lit and threw a circle of light on the plain, scrubbed, white deal table. Seated facing each other were Weekes and his wife, their hands showing, their faces lost in the gloom outside the periphery of lamplight. Both were reading; or at least pretending to do so. No sound save the steady tick of the wall-clock, the breathing of the silent pair, the occasional rustle of a turning page, the chirp and scuffle of mice behind the skirting-board. Mrs. Weekes was reading the Bible. Her lips moved noiselessly.

Hide not thy face from me in the time of my trouble: incline thine ear unto me when I call; O hear me, and that right soon.

> For my days are consumed away like smoke: and my bones are burnt up as it were a fire-brand.
>
> My heart is smitten down and withered like grass: so that I forget to eat my bread...
>
> Mine enemies revile me all the day long: and they that are mad upon me are sworn together against me.

The woman raised her burning eyes and looked across at the man. He had a grey bullet head, a clean-shaven face with grey side-whiskers, a pale, unhealthy face, unusual in a farmer but, together with the watery blue eyes and their heavily pouched sockets, plainly indicative of liver disease. He wore spectacles, purchased from a sixpenny store and which, unsuited to his eyes, caused him to strain to read through them. He peered over them, feeling his wife's gaze upon him. His eyes fell. He dared not look fully at her. He was counting the minutes. It was seven-thirty. As the clock struck ten, she would rise and prepare to retire, at the same time unlocking the corner cupboard which contained his whisky bottle. She would take out the bottle and glass and hand them to him so that he could take his nightcap. He would take the bottle to bed and she would say nothing. By morning, it would be empty. Then, he would have to wait until the next night at ten again. If he wanted a drink between times, he would have to walk to Evingdon. She had forbidden the landlord of "The Bell" and the local storekeeper to serve him. They always did as she told them. He counted for nothing. The clock ticked on. Weekes glanced down at his book. He had bought it for threepence on a barrow at Evingdon fair. It was a rebound copy in black, like a hymn-book. He thought she didn't know what it was. He glanced at the open page furtively.

"Thereupon the Duke's accomplice whipped out a halter, which he had brought with him for the purpose, threw it round Ciuriaci's neck, drew it so tight that he could not utter a sound, and then, with the Duke's aid, strangled him. All this was accomplished as the Duke knew full well, without awakening any in the palace, not even the lady, whom he now approached with a light, and holding it over the bed gently uncovered her person, as she lay fast asleep, and surveyed her from head to foot with no small satisfaction; for fair as she seemed to him dressed, he found her unadorned charms incomparably greater..."

The woman opposite, her face like a mask, was laughing wildly, silently, inside her. She knew full well what that volume from the devil's library held. Had it been any other man, she would have taken and torn it to shreds and consigned it to the fire as a destroyer of souls. As it was...

Weekes could not rest. He watched the minute-finger of the clock moving at slower than snail's pace; he turned his dim eyes to the book... unadorned charms... the smiling face, gleaming teeth, bright eyes of Polly Druce rose before him, faded, and were replaced by a glass and bottle. He was consumed by his appetites. He played with his fingers, cracked the joints, prayed hopelessly in his heart for mercy, before he should be finally lost... damned. There was a double knock on the door. The man started and made as if to rise. The woman gestured to him to remain seated with a commanding wave of the hand. Quietly she laid aside her glasses, marked her page with an embroidered ribbon, carefully closed the book and rose, stiff and straight, to answer the knocking. Her feet pattered down the tiled passage, chains and a bolt raided. Voices at the door. One word reached the listening man. Police. He drew in his breath with a gasp and emitted it again in a distressed whine. He looked wildly around, seeking a refuge and finding none. Littlejohn entered the semi-darkness from the complete blackness outside. Weekes sighed, it seemed with relief. The spell was broken, at last. Anything to break the horror of that boding atmosphere.

Weekes eyed the detective shiftily, but his wife showed no sign of emotion. She bade their visitor take a seat and herself sat down after Littlejohn had introduced himself and brief greetings had passed. The three of them were ranged round the kitchen table like the members of a directors'-meeting, but the way they had settled themselves, the woman with her toilworn but clean hands perfectly controlled and resting on her closed book; Weekes his fingers fumbling with his spectacles, their case and his disguised volume of The Decameron; Littlejohn his large, useful looking fists folded over his pipe on the clean boards; they looked like the sitters at a seance, expecting at any moment a message of rappings from the table. Mrs. Weekes broke the silence.

"A visit from the police is most unusual at this time, Inspector. We're almost ready for bed. We've to get up early in the mornings," she said stiffly.

"I'm sorry to be so late, but I've had a busy day and have only just found the time. It's about the murder of Miss Tither. By the way, I saw you at the graveside this afternoon, Mrs. Weekes."

Weekes started and looked questioningly at his wife, who ignored both him and the detective's remark.

"I don't see how we are concerned. We'd little to do with her and certainly had no cause to wish her dead," she snapped in an acid voice.

"Still, is it not true that there was a quarrel between you, Mrs. Weekes, the last time Miss Tither was here?"

"What do you mean?"

"Miss Tither recently called for her usual basket of crab-apples, I understand, but returned without them. She also informed a certain person in the village that you had told her that she deserved to die for what she had said that day. Is that true?"

"I admit that we had a difference of opinion during her visit. I didn't mention killing her. I merely told her that 'the mouth of them that speak lies shall be stopped!'"

"What was the difference of opinion about?"

"I prefer not to discuss it with you."

Weekes was growing uncomfortable. He glanced anxiously at the clock and then at his wife. "Perhaps you'd like a drink, Inspector," he muttered in wheedling fashion.

"No thanks, Mr. Weekes. Now, Mrs. Weekes please. I'm waiting. I hope you're not going to impede the search for the criminal by withholding what might be vital information."

"I have nothing to say."

"I must warn you, Mrs. Weekes, your attitude is a strange one and likely to be misinterpreted to your disadvantage."

"The affair was private and concerns nobody but me."

Weekes gazed wild-eyed at his wife. His nerves were stretched to breaking-point. Littlejohn caught his glance and realized that if he pursued his course a little longer, Weekes would break down and betray the secret his wife was trying to keep.

"Mrs. Weekes, perhaps you'll tell me where you were then at the time Miss Tither was murdered. Say, between ten and twelve on Wednesday last."

"I have no alibi, if that's what you're after. I was here, busy in the kitchen with cooking. We have no maid and my husband was in the fields. I was alone all that time. But I tell you, I was nowhere near Miss Tither, let alone doing her violence. I am not one to take vengeance in my hands. Vengeance is of the Lord."

"Uhuh. Now, Mr. Weekes, and what of you? Where were you at the same time?"

The farmer tugged at his collar and his eyes roved wildly about, as though seeking again for a place of retreat.

"I was out and about my fields. Nobody see me either."

"Can *you* tell me what occurred during Miss Tither's visit here?"

"I don't know, I tell 'ee. I don't know. Why be you bothering us? We be quiet folk and don't like disturbances. Leave us alone, for God's sake."

Littlejohn played his card.

"Was Miss Tither here to speak about Polly Druce, Mr. Weekes?"

The woman drew her breath sharply, like one drinking noisily. Weekes looked ready to collapse.

"I know all this is distressing, but it's bound to come out. Better tell me in private rather than have it dragged out in public later. Well, I'm waiting."

"I have nothing to say to you," said Mrs. Weekes. She rose, gathered up her Bible and glasses, and looked keenly at her husband. "Miss Tither's slanderous remarks concerned Weekes. If he cares to tell you—and I see he's getting ready to do so—he can. I'm going to the buttery. I've things to attend to."

She left the room stiffly, with long, purposeful strides and closed the door without another word.

Littlejohn turned to the man. "Well, Mr. Weekes?" he said.

The farmer, panic-stricken, was seeking to avoid what he knew was inevitable. "I'm not well to-night, Inspector. I'll call at the police station and tell 'ee all to-morrow. As God's my judge, I will."

"Come, come, Mr. Weekes. You're not going to be convicted of a crime, you know. All I want to know is, what caused the quarrel during Miss Tither's visit here? It was Polly Druce, I know, but I want some details. Now, you can speak freely. The girl's being married to-morrow, so you can put the past behind you."

A startling change had come over Weekes. He rose to his feet, leaned over the table towards Littlejohn and thrust out his loose jaw.

"Say that agen. Married, did 'ee say? It's a lie! A goddam lie! She's mine..." He stopped suddenly, realizing wherein he had betrayed himself. For the first time, a light glowed in his dead eyes. He looked around the room as though not realizing where he was. "Married, you say. Who told you? Out with it, because it's not true. She'd have told me herself. Yes, yes, yes. I bin carryin' on with her. That's what Tither had the row about. Tried to bring me to repentance and when I tell'd her to mind her own business, she up and told the wife, bold as brass. As if the wife didn't know. Punished me for it, too, she 'ave... Look at me. Once I was a fine upstandin' feller. Now a drink-soaked sinner. Can you blame me, seekin' a woman to love? For years and years, we've been sittin' here, night after night, never a word, readin', glarin', getting on one another's nerves. Her lookin' down on me, because I come from peasant stock and hadn't no schoolin'. Then I found Polly… She'm the only one who cared about old Weekes…"

"Well, I had the news from the rector, Mr. Weekes. She's being married by special license to-morrow to young Elliman."

Weekes took a grip on himself. It was evident that Littlejohn's information had at last sunk into his comprehension. "Then, I didn't mean anything to her after all… she just wanted me for the pretty things I'd buy her… well, well. I may as well tell you, then. It was on account of her that I killed Ethel Tither…"

"You?…" exclaimed Littlejohn. Here was a bombshell, indeed. In his ponderings over the case, Littlejohn had suspected one after another, including the vicar himself, but never the whisky-soaked specimen now standing before him, looking more a man than he had previously done.

"Yes. I killed Ethel Tither. You might as well hear it all now. While Polly was mine, or while I thought 'er mine, there was somethin' to live for. Now I'd better be dead… get meself hung and be done with it."

Every Scotland Yard man has had experience of perfectly inno-cent people who morbidly confess to crime, either from despair or some other mental kink. Littlejohn regarded Weekes's statement with reserve and was not prepared to believe it in its bald form.

"You'd better tell me what this is all about, Mr. Weekes, and I must warn you that anything you may say may be used in evidence later. Perhaps you'd prefer to come with me to the police station and sign a statement."

"Later. First let me get it off my conscience, then I'll sign. God forgive me. I been a sinner, I knows. But I did pray and wrestle

agen the powers o' darkness. But never a light or an answer to
my prayers came. Only Mrs. Weekes, 'ating and condemning me.
I'm a lost man. The Lord 'a mercy on my soul. Come to think of
it, I've got little to say. Tither called to see me here. I must leave
Polly Druce alone, or take the consequences. Which meant, she
said, she'd not only tell my wife, but the squire and his lady and
get Polly disgraced. I tell'd Tither to go to 'ell, in the white heat
of rage. She left me some tracts, which I didn't read, but put in
my pocket. Well, she told my wife and told the squire, too. Polly
told me on Monday as she'd got her notice from milady. I told
Polly I'd see her all right. Told 'er I'd see Tither, too, and give her
a piece o' my mind. It must be getting the sack as made Polly
marry young Elliman. He was always hangin' round 'er afore he
joined-up. But she'd rather 'ave me in those days. On account of
my money, I guess. Well…"

Weekes swallowed hard, turned to the corner cupboard, tried
the door, and, finding it locked, was seized with sudden rage and
tore it open, smashing the lock. He extracted a bottle and glass,
filled the latter half-full of whisky, and drank it off.

"That's better. Have a drink, Inspector?"

"No, thanks."

"Well, I'd bin on the look-out for Miss Tither, just to give her
a piece of my mind. I'd also got one of her tracts, with the worst
word I knew written on it, just to show her I didn't care. On
Wednesday morning, I see her—just about eleven it would be,—I
see her crossing the Evingdon road to the short cut across the
vicarage field. I wuz on the Evingdon road, too, so I hurried along
an' caught her up, just half-way across the field. I asks her what
she bin up to and says, 'as fer your tracts, take that.' And I hands

her the one I'd wrote on. She didn't even look at it. Clutched it in her palm and let fly at me, abusing me, like. I could take that all right and I give her as much as she gave me. I tell'd her a thing or two, I'll tell 'ee. But when she started about Polly, I jest seemed to see red. 'Yew say another word about her and I'll smack ye across the mouth and stop yer lies,' I sez. This made her worse. I forgot myself. I'd a hoe in my hand—I'd been spudding out thistles in my meadow—and afore I knew what I was at, I up and strikes her with the heavy handle of it. In my rage, I hit harder than I intended. She jest fell over and lay still."

"Was there anybody about at the time?"

"Not a soul, as I see. I couldn't leave 'er there in the middle of the field. I looked at 'er. She didn't move. I felt her and she was like a corpse. I'd killed 'er. I lost me head. I picked her up and carried her to the hedge and lay her under it."

"What part of the hedge?"

"By the gap in the trees, just through by the vicarage. I left her there because I didn't know what else to do. All I could hope for was that I'd not been seen. Perhaps, I thought, they'll think she was kicked by a horse, or some'at. Then, I sneaked off as fast as I could and started spudding thistles in my field to give myself as good an alibi as I could. But it doesn't do, Inspector. Murder will out. Blood cries from the ground. I'm beat. God forgive me."

"Do you mean to tell me you left the body there and didn't put it in the vicarage cesspool?"

"Cesspool? What's that to do with it?"

"Don't you read the papers? Haven't you heard the gossip or about the inquest, man?"

"No. I stopped my ears to all talk or anything else about the murder from outside. I knew she'd been found, but I wanted to hear no more. I heard enough about it night and day from my own conscience."

"You didn't know, then, that Miss Tither was found in Mr. Claplady's cesspit? The traces of your blow were discovered on her head, but she didn't die from it. She was drowned in the water of the pit after being thrown in by someone who found her after you left her."

Weekes' eyes almost popped from his head. "Then, I'm not a murderer? I didn't kill her?"

"No. But you'd better come with me to the station. We must take this down and you must give us a statement before witnesses. Come along now, please. Get your things."

Weekes rose, looking as though a burden had been lifted from his shoulders. He made for the door through which his wife had departed, leaving it open. Littlejohn could hear him clattering about in the scullery, apparently putting on his boots. The detective buttoned his coat. He would be glad to be on his way and out of the terrible atmosphere of hate which seemed to pervade the whole of Upper Hilary Farm. Suddenly, there was an ear-splitting explosion. Littlejohn hurled himself in the direction whence it came. He was too late. Weekes was lying on the red-tiled floor of the little room; by his side a shot gun. He was not a pleasant sight, for he had apparently put the barrels to his temple. The Inspector raised his head at the sound of a noise above. A staircase rose from a dim corner of the scullery and at the top stood Mrs. Weekes, holding a candle aloft. She had on a long nightgown with a heavy coat thrown hastily over it. She was still prim and forbidding, even in her deshabille and the light of the candle distorted her features grotesquely.

"Whatever is it?" she asked, peering down into the gloom, illuminated only by a small kitchen lamp.

"Your husband has shot himself, Mrs. Weekes. Better get dressed and come down at once." Afterwards, Littlejohn realized that he had expressed no sympathy. It did not seem called for in that house of hate.

Mrs. Weekes stood stiffly at the stairhead for a second or two. Then, suddenly, her body seemed to sag and grow limp. With a wild cry, she reeled forward and fell from top to bottom of the stairs and lay still.

CHAPTER XII

Ropewalker Street

DETECTIVE-SERGEANT CROMWELL WATCHED THE CITY streets sailing past him from his seat on the top of a No. 11 bus and then, satisfied that he was near his destination, ran nimbly downstairs, seized the rail, launched himself into space, landed sedately on both feet and walked on calmly, unperturbed by the conductor's flow of strong remonstrance. Ropewalker Street is one of a maze of rather wide thoroughfares running parallel to Liverpool Street and consists largely of blocks of offices inhabited by every description of trade and profession, ranging from coathanger makers and furriers to accountants, actuaries and even dentists. Halting before a nondescript building half-way along the street, the detective began to read the names on the tablet at the door and then turned in. To his disgust, there was no lift and he was compelled to walk up three flights of depressing stairs before reaching the office he was seeking. He halted before a glass door at the end of a small corridor at the back of the block. A cheap tenement—probably one of the cheapest in the building. On the panel, the words "HOME GOSPEL ALLIANCE". Cromwell straightened his face into its most solemn expression and knocked on the door. He was a very suitable officer for paying such a visit, for, swollen with innocent pride at the name he bore, he had a puritanical outlook and tried to behave under all circumstances as he thought his great namesake, The Protector, would have done.

There was a scuffling in the room as though someone were either hastily concealing something, or else assembling a mass of papers and books on a desk to make himself look very busy.

"Come in," called a voice.

Cromwell found himself in a small, dusty office. Ragged carpet on the floor, battered blinds at the windows, stacks of sunburned Bibles and hymn-books on the window-sills. A battered typewriter on a table under the window. A desk, which had seen better days, in the middle of the room, littered with printed papers and ledgers, a bottle of yellow-looking water and a dusty glass, a cash-box, an attache-case, a bowler hat and an apple. The mantelpiece was a mass of tracts and over it was a framed document which looked like a list of rules and regulations for bringing sinners to repentance. Seated at the desk was a heavy man, with sagging features, a large hooked nose, small dark eyes and a thick, tousled head of grey hair. He rose to greet his visitor, who was impressed by his huge bulk and air of unctuous shiftiness.

"Good morning, sir, and what can I do for you?" said the man whom Cromwell, who had a strange weakness for christening people he met with names he imagined were suitable, had mentally labelled Mr. Wuthering Heights.

"Mr. Mortimore, I presume?"

"Yes."

"My name is Cromwell, Robert Cromwell," said the detective, refusing to change his surname under any circumstances. "I'm interested in your Society, sir. I give a tenth of my income every year to deserving causes and wouldn't like to overlook any worthy aim. Perhaps you'll give me some particulars to guide me."

Wuthering Heights began to bustle around with remarkable agility for one so heavy. He bowed Cromwell into the only other chair in the room, he rummaged in drawers and cabinets, he walked up and down the room enlarging on the labours and objects of his Society, and finally, handed his visitor a sheaf of papers containing details of the number of fallen women, drunkards, thieves and rogues rescued from perdition over a period of years, a dozen or more slips of paper to be filled up by subscribers, and a large form for use by those desirous of leaving legacies to the Alliance.

"Of course," said Mr. Mortimore, after describing the work done by his staff of missioners and the haunts in which it was carried out, "of course, this little office is only the centre, the ahem—control-room—of a vast organization. Here the work is reported, organized, checked and financed. This is the heart, let us say, the heart whence is pumped the life-blood of the whole body. Our limbs embrace every part of the country. In fact, at this moment, our chief, Dr. Scarisdale, is carrying on an urgent work in the slums of Scotland. I myself, was once in the front line of battle, and believe me, my friend, it's exhilarating, a fine work! Failing health, however, ties me to my desk and I do what I can, I do what I can."

"If I include your Society in my list of donations, however," interposed Cromwell, looking as sanctimonious as Wuthering Heights himself, "I shall require evidence that the funds are usefully and correctly applied."

"I appreciate your scrupulousness, Mr. Cromwell. One has to be careful these days. I can let you have, annually, our audited balance-sheet, drawn up by a firm of reputable accountants and showing a list of the various fields of labour. I take it that such a warranty would be satisfactory?"

"Yes, I think it would. But tell me, how is it your Society is not more widely known? I'd never heard of it until, the other day, a friend, who desired to remain an anonymous well-wisher to you, told me about your splendid work."

"We are, Mr. Cromwell, we are what I might call, a private society. Work of this kind must be conducted with discretion. It's not like a public hospital, or a child or animal welfare organization. It deals with lives which, though broken, still retain elements of pride and spirit, and to make a lot of publicity about our labours might seriously detract from their usefulness. We are, therefore, mainly supported by a limited circle of well-doers and although we could do more with larger funds, we prefer to pursue our present policy. You follow?"

"Oh, yes, yes, yes. I quite follow you. And now this firm of accountants. Forgive me, but if I'm to contribute—and I may say, substantially,—I want the fullest information. This firm of account-ants, Chitty, Mulliner and Passey, I've never heard of 'em before..."

"Oh, tut, tut, tut, sir. One of the best firms in the City. Warranted Accountants, all of them. Absolutely undoubted. They're in this building—bottom floor—and are of the highest repute."

"Well, I'm much obliged to you, Mr. Mortimore, and I'll very favourably consider supporting your cause. I hope it will continue to prosper and find rich harvests for the reaping." And with that, Cromwell rose and allowed himself to be purred over and bowed out by Wuthering Heights, who was beginning to get on his nerves. When he reached the second floor, Cromwell underwent a slight metamorphosis. He rolled up his umbrella smartly, slewed his hat to a more jaunty angle, unfastened his coat button, and slid his hand nonchalantly into his trousers pocket. With the other hand, he took from another pocket a card inscribed "Cromwell's Directories... represented by R. Cromwell, director." Armed with this, he entered the swing doors of Chitty, Mulliner and Passey on the ground floor and rang the bell for attention.

The place seemed deserted, but from somewhere behind a closed glass shutter Cromwell could hear pattering feet and soon the head of a lady, forty years or thereabouts and annoyed at being disturbed, was thrust forth.

"Good morning," said Cromwell and presented his card.

"We don't want any directories," answered the sour-faced lady and closed the shutter.

"Wait a minute, madam," said the detective, "I'm not trying to sell you anything. I'm here seeking information."

The shutter opened again and the long-toothed attendant once more thrust out her face. "Why didn't you say so at first, then?"

"I'm making an annual revision of our directory, madam, and naturally you wouldn't like your firm to be missed, or wrongly described, now would you?"

"I've never heard of Cromwell's Directories before," said the lady suspiciously and still sour-faced.

"What! Never heard of Cromwell's? I *am* surprised. We've a very large circulation in the best circles."

"Well, please state your business. It's getting near my lunch-time."

"May I see Mr. Chitty, Mr. Mulliner or Mr. Passey, please?"

"A lot you know about this firm! They've all been dead this ten years or more. Mr. Theodore Jenkinson is now sole partner of the business."

"Is he in?"

"No. He's out of town on an audit. You see, since he took over this concern about eight years ago, he's gradually retired from it. Why, I don't know. Why bother to buy it and then let the audits drift away one by one, I can't think. When Mr. Chitty was alive, we'd enough work to keep a staff of fifteen occupied. Now there's only Mr. Jenkinson and me. He's never troubled to replace the clients we've lost and now there aren't enough to keep one man busy. Mr. Jenkinson does all the work that comes and that doesn't keep him fully going. All the same, my job's comfortable and I get good pay, so it suits me."

"Quite, quite. I'm obliged to you. I think you've given me enough information to be going on with. By the way, Mr. Jenkinson is a member of the Society of Warranted Accountants, isn't he?"

"Yes."

"I'm grateful to you for your help. Let me see, what's your name? I must send you one of our diaries at Christmas."

"Miss Livermore," came the answer, rather more graciously than before.

Cromwell made a note of it and bidding the lady good-bye, hastened to the street. Thence, he made his way to Gresham Street and turned into the ornamental portals of the Society of Warranted Accountants. He was civilly received by the Assistant Secretary, Mr. Peover, to whom he explained his true business.

"Oh, deary me," said Mr. Peover, thumbing his chin apprehensively. "Not another financial scandal brewing, I hope. I've only just recovered from one."

"No, I think not. I'm just enquiring concerning the present

proprietor of Chitty, Mulliner and Passey, a Mr. Jenkinson. Can you tell me anything about him?"

Mr. Peover took down a book of reference and pored over it through the heavy, pebbled spectacles he wore. To look straight at his eyes was like gazing into a pool into which a stone had been thrown, such an optical commotion did his cataract lenses seem to create. He ran a careful finger down columns of names.

"Ah, h'm. Here we are. Theodore Jenkinson, Certified Member, 1908. That's a long time ago. First employed with Jeremiah Titmuss, F.W.A., Trentbridge. That was 1908 to 1914. Then he vanished for a time. Perhaps in the army. Here he is, back again on the Roll in 1932, as sole partner in Chitty, Mulliner and Passey. That was a good firm in the old days, but the principals died one by one and, finally, their trustees sold what was left of the goodwill to Mr. Jenkinson. He doesn't do much, from what I hear. Mainly charity audits, I think."

"Thanks very much, Mr. Peover. That's very helpful. You'll keep this visit strictly confidential, won't you? Trentbridge, you said Mr. Jenkinson started at, eh?"

Mr. Peover agreed, shook hands with his visitor and bade him call again if he needed further help. At the same time he gave Cromwell an admiring glance, which, passing through the powerful lenses, was transformed into a ferocious glare, which left Cromwell somewhat at a loss to understand what was really in Mr. Peover's mind.

This part of his work finished, Detective-Sergeant Cromwell adjourned to a café, ordered two poached eggs on two rounds of toast, a doughnut, a pot of tea and a large mixed ice, and whilst his order was being made up by a disdainful young lady, he put through a call to "The Bell" at Hilary from the public call-box. Just as he had been informed by the landlord there that Littlejohn was out and his destination unknown, the disappointed Cromwell's first course arrived. The waitress glared at him for daring to vacate his table. Cromwell gingerly raised the thin covering of white-of-egg from his toast and his features grew grim. The underpart of each slice was coal-black and pretence had not even been made of scraping it. "Hey!" he called to the scornful one and beneath the goggling eyes of several elderly business men, whose blandishments were responsible for her haughty demeanour, declined, without thanks, to eat his eggs on charcoal, rose, left the place in dudgeon and transferred his custom to a neighbouring competitor, who served him with as much as he could eat for one-and-eight.

Over a buck rabbit (with two rounds, twopence extra), Cromwell pondered his next step. Valuable time might be wasted if he hung about for further orders from Littlejohn. Whenever faced by a poser, Cromwell always asked himself one question. "What would Oliver Cromwell have done?" Bold improvisation, that was it! He called for a timetable and was informed that there wasn't such a thing in the place. Try Cook's in Cheapside. At 1.30, he was at Euston and 5.0 o'clock found him in Trentbridge enquiring at the police station if they knew anyone of the name of Titmuss.

The sergeant on duty smiled forlornly. He was a huge, red-faced man with a heavy, sandy moustache and he had never served elsewhere than in Trentbridge. He had seen time, like an ever-rolling stream, bearing all its sons in Trentbridge away in one fashion or another, and being of a melancholy disposition, he wondered when his own turn would come. His drawer in the charge-room desk was filled with patent medicines of all kinds. Sadly he gazed on Cromwell.

"Titmuss, did you say? Out of business these dozen years or more. A fine connection. Largest accountants in the place. Three brothers. Two dead. Cut off in their prime. The other, Mr. Edwin, still lives up top o' the town, but he's wheeled out in a bath-chair. Parilized, from the waist down, on account of a stroke. Business fizzled out arter that…"

Apprehensively, the huge policeman opened a drawer, extracted a blood-pressure pill and swallowed it with a laborious gulp.

"Can you give me Mr. Edwin Titmuss's address?"

The sergeant-in-charge hastily consulted a telephone directory.

"Lives at a viller in Oxford Road, that's up top o' the town. Foller the tram-lines up the hill and where they turns left, you turns right. Name of viller is… is… wot's this? Cham… Chamy… wot the…?"

"Spell it out."

"'c-h-a-m-o-n-i-x,'" rumbled the sergeant hesitantly.

"Oh, Chamonicks… South o' France…" said Cromwell wisely. "Thanks. I'll be off then. Appreciate your help. Good-bye."

"Be seein' yer…" said the doleful sergeant. He could never persuade himself to say good-bye to anybody. It sounded too final. Meditatively, he slipped a soda-mint in his mouth.

Mr. Edwin Titmuss, a pink-faced, white-haired, well-groomed man, was sitting in the garden of "Chamonix", his legs and feet swathed in rugs, a copy of *The Countryman* and a pair of binoculars on his lap. He greeted his visitor genially.

"I've just been watching the sparrows at the bottom of the lawn settling a family difference," he said, chuckling, and then, realizing that Cromwell had not come to study bird life, asked him his business.

"But first, let us have a drink," said the jovial invalid and taking up a small silver whistle, tied round his neck by a silk cord, he blew a short blast on it. A neat maid appeared through the french window and served iced lager at his bidding. "Now," said Mr. Titmuss, after they had sampled and approved their beer.

"I'm seeking information about a certain Theodore Jenkinson, who, I gather, was at one time articled to you. Do you remember him, sir?"

"Dear me… delving back into the dim past, aren't you? Yes, I think I can help, Mr. Cromwell. You see, I've been almost helpless for many years and one who can't get about much in the present, must enjoy many things in retrospect. To kill time, I've made a study of the birds of my garden and also written up my diaries for almost a lifetime. The bird life has been the subject of a small monograph which I've published. You must remind me to give you a copy before you leave. The past life of Edwin Titmuss, however, has not been published, but I'll give you some extracts relevant to what you're seeking…"

Mr. Titmuss blew another shrill blast on his little whistle. In response to very precise instructions concerning volumes and dates, the pretty maid left them and returned with two black books, resembling morocco Bibles, which she handed to her master. Mr. Titmuss turned over the pages, reading extracts and Cromwell jotted down details in his notebook. Finally, the subject exhausted, the two men settled down to afternoon tea, which Mr. Titmuss insisted on having served. During that meal, Cromwell succumbed to the charm of a delightful old man, who talked of past events and of the present affairs of his friends, the birds. They got on so well together, that the detective left not only with a small book on *The Birds in my Garden*, by Edwin Titmuss, but also a pair of field-glasses and two standard works on ornithology. Thus, Cromwell of Scotland Yard turned bird-watcher, ceased to model his life on that of his more famous namesake, and became himself. Henceforth, his holidays were spent between certain spots haunted by birds and the back garden of "Chamonix", Trentbridge. The work, *Birds of the Backyard and Beyond*, by Titmuss and Cromwell, is highly thought of among amateur ornithologists…

Back in his rooms in Knightsbridge, Cromwell on the night of his first encounter with Mr. Titmuss, collated and arranged the notes he had gathered on Theodore Jenkinson. Just after midnight, he had before him the following précis, which he enclosed with a brief note in an envelope and posted to Littlejohn at the Bell Inn, Hilary Magna.

Theodore Jenkinson, born about 1882 at (?). Educated local Grammar School. Entered Bank of Trentbridge, 1898. "There he tried to teach the manager how to conduct his business and his services were dispensed with." Entered firm of Titmuss, 1900. Passed final accountancy exams., 1908. Remained with Titmuss until 1914, when he joined the army. Mr. Titmuss heard from him several times. He was demobilized in 1919, after reaching rank of Major. Served: France, Italy, Rhineland. Nothing further heard of him until he set up on his own by buying almost defunct business of Chitty, Mulliner and Passey of London, 1932. Nothing more known of career.

Character, etc. Clever. Scholarship boy at school. Active brain, ambitious, with ideas above his station. Hence his quarrel with his first employers. Seemed to settle down with Mr. Titmuss, who promised him a partnership if he behaved and was diligent. Just before outbreak of war in 1914, showed decided signs of restlessness and talked of launching-out in London. His quick brain gained him rapid promotion in the army and he was attached to Headquarters. This gave impetus to his ambition and high-flown notions. Mr. Titmuss's expectations that he would never return to Trentbridge were fulfilled.

Family. Son of an under-park-keeper employed by Trentbridge Corporation, Lemuel Jenkinson. Very respect-able and religious people. Jenkinson, senior, arrived at Trentbridge from the country, where he had been an estate gardener, with two children, a boy and a girl. Theodore aged about eleven, girl (name forgotten), aged thirteen. Lemuel returned to his native place—*Hilary Magna*—when Theodore started in the bank, leaving the lad in lodgings. The mother died during their stay in Trentbridge and the sister kept house afterwards. She and her brother seemed very attached. Mr. Titmuss met her when he took on her brother, as she was visiting Trentbridge in search of new lodgings for him. Described as a "plain, masterful, little thing", and was in service at some country house near her home.

Attached is a photograph of Mr. Titmuss and staff taken during their annual trip, 1913, to Hunstanton. Jenkinson is the third man from the left, front row. This is almost thirty years old, but may prove useful.

*

Satisfied with his day's work and his literary effort, Cromwell ate his supper and, taking a copiously illustrated book on birds to bed with him, lighted his pipe and settled down for a quiet browse and smoke. The following morning, he got into trouble with his landlady for burning a hole in what she exaggeratedly described as one of her best linen sheets. Glad that nothing worse had arisen from his falling asleep with a red-hot pipe between his teeth, Cromwell paid up with a smile.

CHAPTER XIII

A Surprise over Afternoon Tea

S UNDAY BROUGHT A HALT TO LITTLEJOHN'S INVESTIGATIONS, for Hilary takes its day of rest seriously. Not that, on the Sunday in question, everyone relaxed. The death of Weekes of Upper Hilary Farm was news early in the morning and Harriwinckle, Oldfield, the doctor, a group of pressmen and a swarm of hangers-on toiled like slaves and put in a full day's work before lunch. At the same time, Polly Druce was running a rival show by getting married at nine in the morning. In addition, it was Harvest Thanksgiving Day. Small wonder that the bewildered Mr. Claplady, at the morning service, announced a hymn praying for rain, instead of setting his flock to plough the fields and scatter. The Methodist Harvest Home was in full swing as Polly and her new husband were borne off to a wedding-feast in Evingdon—"The Bell" not having sufficient rations at so short a notice—and "Come, ye thankful people, COME", emitted from the tin tabernacle at the cross-roads, could be heard far beyond the village boundaries.

As far as carrying on with the Tither case, Littlejohn found it advisable to call a short halt, for having been on the premises at Upper Hilary Farm at the time of the tragedy there, he was the principal witness and much of his time was taken up in consultations with his colleagues of the local force and the doctor. The coroner was away for the week-end, but his officer provisionally fixed the inquest for the following Tuesday. Meanwhile, Mrs. Weekes had recovered, with little more than a few bruises, from her fall downstairs, and answered questions and attended to the work of her small farm, her sour face set like a block of granite, her features betraying no emotion whatever. There was nothing to suggest that Weekes's death was anything other than suicide, and the inquest was expected to confirm that opinion. The state of health of the man, his drinking habits, his highly nervous, melancholy condition, with the final thunderclaps of his assault on Miss Tither and Polly Druce's wedding, were regarded as ample motives for the act.

It was afternoon before Littlejohn found himself freed from the formalities arising out of the death of Weekes and, after Oldfield and his collaborators had gone back to Evingdon, the Scotland Yard man decided to explore the village and neighbourhood, hoping that a brisk walk in the pleasant country around would take his mind from the case and bring him back fresh to it afterwards. He therefore lit his pipe, borrowed a stout ash-plant from the landlord of "The Bell", and strode off along the Hilary Parva road in search of the humbler satellite of the village in which he was staying. Briar Cottage, as he passed it, showed no signs of life except smoke rising from one chimney, although Mr. Wynyard was still in residence there. Presumably, he was keeping house in mournful seclusion; Littlejohn could not imagine him thanksgiving with the rest of the village under the circumstances. The detective paused to admire the trimness of Holly Bank and turning, was surprised to find that he had imperceptibly climbed a gentle hill and that, from the rising land where he stood, he had a view of the meadow in which Miss Tither had met her death.

From the gateway of Holly Bank, he could see between "The Bell" and a row of cottages, the upper half of the fatal field ranging from the footpaths to the Evingdon road. From the upper windows of Lorrimer's house, one would probably overlook the exact scene of the crime. As he pondered his discovery, Littlejohn heard footsteps and turning, found Lorrimer himself approaching from the village.

"Good afternoon, Inspector. Admiring the view?" said the dapper man, smiling inquisitively. "It certainly is a pretty scene from this slope. An even better sight from the windows of my place, which, standing as it does on a bank, has a full panorama."

"I was just thinking, Mr. Lorrimer, that anyone looking from the windows of your house would have in sight the full scene of Miss Tither's murder."

"I agree. The thought struck me at once. A pity someone wasn't watching when the blow was struck. It would have saved you a lot of trouble. As you know, however, my small staff was occupied at the time preparing a meal and I was at the piano... Care to come in for a cup of tea? By the way, this Weekes business is a shocking affair, isn't it, although it's perhaps as well that it's happened this way? Had Weekes waited for nature, I'm afraid the road would have been long and painful. He was pickled in alcohol, you know, and the end of hob-nailed-liver sufferers is, as a rule, most distressing. I feel damned sorry for his wife. A decent little woman, who's suffered no end from her husband's shiftless ways. And the fellow was carrying on, too, with that Druce girl who's been married this morning—the strumpet!"

Lorrimer was becoming quite animated and Littlejohn, having his mind set on his walk and determined not to be led into an hour or two of gossip, excused himself and went his way. He was surprised at Lorrimer's interest in other people's affairs, especially those of Mrs. Weekes, who seemed to have few friends in the village.

Past the gates of Hilary Hall, with its parkland and fine old trees, between thick spinneys which flanked the highway and through which it had apparently been cut, to the hamlet,—it could hardly be called a village,—of Hilary Parva. It was a pleasant spot, with a small row of four whitewashed, wattle-and-daub cottages, built deeply in gardens, a beer-house and the rather imposing brick church, erected to rival that of the larger village by a one-time crazy lord of the manor, whose former residence, standing in grounds at the end of the hamlet, had been bought and converted into a convalescent home by a trade union. The church was closed. Mr. Claplady only attended there on odd occasions, the church at Hilary Magna serving both places, as a rule. A few cottagers hung about their houses and patients could be seen taking the air in the large, well-kept park of the converted manor. Taking a by-road, Littlejohn found himself on the Evingdon-Stretton Harcourt road and in a quarter of an hour more, was passing the lane which led to Upper Hilary Farm. A stream of motor traffic spoiled much of the pleasure of walking on this highway and Littlejohn was beginning to wish that he had continued straight ahead from Hilary Parva, when an idea struck him. He was feeling ready for a cup of tea. What better place to take it in than Miss Satchell's tea-rooms farther along the Stretton road, past the Methodist Chapel, which was enjoying a tea interval, preparatory to resuming activities in the evening? A group of whole-day worshippers, apparently from more remote places, were refreshing themselves in the small graveyard and beneath a tree were spread carrier-bags, sandwich papers and cups of tea. The partakers of the feast were indulging in various kinds of conversation, ranging from earnest hobnobbing by serious-minded young men and ladies, to frivolous banter between an excited, ancient deacon and a large mutton dressed as a lamb. As Littlejohn passed, the bearded elder was unwillingly resisting the temptation to deliver a hearty slap on the spreading behind of his skittish companion. The detective, puffing his pipe, strolled on, across the bridge spanning the clear little Fenny Brook, to the tea-rooms at the junction of the Stretton Lattimer and Stretton Harcourt roads.

Satchell's tea-rooms consist of a bungalow, which houses the proprietress, a large annexe, where food and drink are served, a car-park, and a small garden, where in summer, brightly-coloured umbrellas protect the complexions of those who wish to eat out-of-doors. Miss Satchell was a middle-aged school-teacher, who tired of her job and bought a moribund road-house for a mere song against the advice of all her friends. The place was on the main road, that was true, but remote from any centre which might harbour enough people willing to pay extravagant prices for bits of things like multicoloured iced buns, tiny scones, muffins, crumpets, cups of coffee and pots of tea. But Miss Satchell made up her mind about the job. In twelve months, she had baked her way to local fame and was on the road to small fortune. At first, she made, prepared and served her own wares. Then, her place was "discovered" by two local county leaders, Miss Phillimore-Cadby and Lady Winstanley. After that, Miss Satchell's future was assured. It became the thing to run out to Satchell's for morning coffee, afternoon tea, light lunch, or even high tea. Cars filled the park; customers filled the tables; Miss Satchell filled the till. She continued to bake her own cakes, but paid other girls to serve them, whilst she, by this time semi-county herself, clad in tweeds, heavy brogues and booming loudly, palavered with her regular customers and called many of them by their first names.

Littlejohn entered the tea-room and managed to find a solitary table in a quiet corner. The place was over-whelmingly "olde Englyshe". Large, open, brick fireplace, carefully laid with logs, and a spinning-wheel by the hearth. Brass of all kinds. Bed-warmers, hot-water cans, trays, candlesticks of all shapes and sizes, splattered on the walls and standing on every available ledge and shelf. Copper cans and jugs; gongs, bells, three grandfather clocks, framed samplers, toby jugs, pot dogs, witch balls, and a hundred-and-one odd antiques, bogus or real, scattered liberally all over the shop. They were all for sale, but Littlejohn did not know or heed that. He asked the pleasant-faced waitress if he could see Miss Satchell and was told that she would be back in ten minutes. The girl indicated through the window that the tweed-covered hindquarters projecting from a sports-car which was just about to depart with Miss Phillimore-Cadby, were those of her mistress. Littlejohn could see the occupant of the car and Miss Satchell bobbing and teething at each other vociferously, as though sharing some choice titbit of local scandal. The detective's scones were sorted out from a towering mass on a counter groaning beneath piles of candies, home-made fudge, peppermint crêmes (exclusive agency), lollipops, muffins, crumpets and doughnuts, and he found them to his tooth as he waited and looked around him.

Timid courting couples, out for the first time, whispering, thrilled, and all-in-all to each other. Blasé young men and girls, manifesting symptoms of arrested development or St. Vitus's Dance, bawling and baying about the place, or treating each other with studied contempt, whilst ignoring the presence and feelings of everybody else. Respectable married couples, out for a little treat and almost apologetic to the noisier element for their presence there. On every hand, eating and drinking. Littlejohn watched his fellow mortals at afternoon tea and joined in the rite. Miss Satchell, tall, middle-aged, heavy limbed, pink-faced, with a mop of untidy, grey hair and twinkling, grey eyes, joined him. She was carrying his card in her hand.

"Inspector Littlejohn? How-do-you-do. You want to see me, I believe."

"Yes. Miss Satchell, I take it? How-do-you-do, madam. It's about Miss Tither's visit here on the morning of her death. You've already told Constable Harriwinckle something about it, but I thought I'd call myself, just in case you'd remembered any other points which you might think of interest. It was certainly help-ful of you to ring up and inform us where Miss Tither was last Wednesday morning, and the purpose of her call here."

"Poor dear. She was a bit of a bore, I'll admit, but she didn't deserve what she got, Inspector. I'm only too willing to help where I can."

Miss Satchell was beginning to enjoy herself, drew up a chair to Littlejohn's table, and became immersed in the matter in hand. She ordered more tea and scones for both of them, a step which the detective welcomed, for his walk had given him an appetite which the trifles he had eaten only stimulated.

"Tell me, Miss Satchell, did you see Miss Tither leaving this place? Which way did she take and was there anyone else about in the road as she went?"

"No, I didn't go to the door with her. You see, we make light lunches, and I'd my hands full at the time clearing-off the coffee and seeing to the twelve o'clock preparations. She paid at the counter, called back to me good-morning, and was gone."

"Was there anyone else about the café who might have seen her cross the road and go through the stile? Perhaps she met someone on the road, too. Can you think who was about the room at the time?"

"There were quite a lot of people here, of course; it was coffee-time when she called. I'm just thinking if anyone in particular was about in the car-park when she left." Miss Satchell paused, with a rock-bun poised halfway between her plate and her mouth.

"Come to think of it, Johnny Hilsborough opened the door for her. Yes, that's it! He was buying some candies at the counter as Miss Tither came to pay her check, they left together, and he held open the door for her. Johnny's your man. Perhaps he passed her in his car. He left right away afterwards, for Evingdon. He's over there. The round, red-faced boy, with the big moustache. I'll get him."

Miss Satchell bounded across the tea-room, followed by a score or more pairs of eyes, and brought back a fair, muscular, good-natured-looking youth to Littlejohn's table.

"This is Inspector Littlejohn, of Scotland Yard, who's investigating the Tither crime, you know. Mr. Johnny Hilsborough, Inspector."

"Good afternoon, Mr. Hilsborough. Good of you to take the trouble to come over."

"Ahjidoo, Inspector. Not a bit o' trouble. Always glad to help the jolly old law, eh, what? Now, sir, what can I do for you?"

"I understand from Miss Satchell, that you saw Miss Tither leaving here on the morning of her death, Mr. Hilsborough."

"Come to think of it, I did see the poor old girl. Opened the door to let her out, in fact, and passed her in my 'bus on my way home. Talkin' at the stile with Lorrimer, the bald-headed bloke who bought the mater's player-piano."

He proudly brushed his large moustache, his childish, blue eyes beaming goodwill and anxiety to help. Littlejohn, who was disposing of the last of his scones, almost choked at the spate of alarming information so blandly volunteered by Hilsborough.

"You mean to say, Mr. Hilsborough, that Miss Tither walked straight from here and met Lorrimer?"

"Yes. The old boy was walking down the road in the direction of the village, probably goin' home. Miss T. overtook him and spoke to him for a minute or two. He seemed in a hurry to be off, though. She went through the stile in the field and old Lorrimer went on by road. I saw old Weekes pottering about the field as Miss Tither crossed it. I was just revving up the old 'bus and after that I didn't see anything else there... By Jove! Miss Tither must have been killed just after... Old Weekes must have been near the spot at the time."

"He was, Mr. Hilsborough. But he died last night, so we'd better leave that point out for the present, please. Now, what is that about a player-piano from your mother? I was at Mr. Lorrimer's house a day or two ago and he'd a grand piano then, not a player."

"Oh yes. The gadget he bought from the mater is a thing you can attach and take off a piano as you wish. It's a thing like a small organ that takes the roll of record thingummyjig, you know, and then you switch on the current and the thing plays by striking the keys of your piano. What I mean to say is that it'll fit on any piano… you get what I'm driving at, don't you?"

"Yes, I quite understand, Mr. Hilsborough…"

"Although what use to you a ruddy player-piano gadget is, in connection with Miss Tither's being bumped-off, I can't quite see. Anyhow, there it is… excuse me, won't you? Don't want me for anything else, eh? Always ready to oblige, but… young lady waitin' at the table there for me… cheerio! Chin, chin, Satchy, old girl…"

"Cheerio! Mr. Hilsborough, and many thanks for your help."

Littlejohn thanked Miss Satchell and rose to pay his bill, which was immediately waved aside. "You're my guest, Inspector, and I'm glad to have met you," said Miss Satchell, bade him good-bye and departed to greet a newcomer.

Here was a staggering discovery! Lorrimer had lied! He had met Miss Tither just before her death, in spite of the fact that he had asserted that he was indoors, playing the piano all morning. Playing the piano! This was confirmed by Mr. Lorrimer's servants. But, the man had a player-piano attachment, which, electrically operated, could be left working and making music, whilst its owner was far from the spot. Then and there, Littlejohn decided that Holly Bank called for another visit and the sooner, the better.

On his way out of Miss Satchell's, Littlejohn ordered two pounds of fudge to be sent to his wife, and paid six shillings for it. Mrs. Littlejohn was delighted with her husband's kindly thought of her at a crucial moment in his case, but, on hearing the price, said he had paid at least four times more than the stuff was worth.

CHAPTER XIV

The Fox Goes to Ground

FROM SATCHELL'S TEA-ROOMS, LITTLEJOHN MADE HIS WAY to Holly Bank again. He had urgent questions to ask Mr. Lorrimer and he felt he wanted the answers at once. He was disappointed, however, for he found the place locked-up. The owner was apparently out and, judging from the smoking chimneys, the servants had banked the fires and taken a Sunday evening off. The detective, therefore, after telephoning to the police station at Evingdon to make an appointment, arranged to meet Oldfield later in the evening. He took a 'bus to the little market town and soon was in conference with his colleague.

"I'm sorry I've spent so little time with you, Littlejohn," said Oldfield, by way of preamble, "but there's so much to do these days, with local A.R.P., two country-house burglaries, and a number of sidelines running at Hilary, such as this new suicide of Old Weekes's. It takes us all our time to keep abreast of things. What are the latest developments?"

Littlejohn gave his friend a brief account of his day's labours, laying particular emphasis on the facts which had come to light at his interview with Hilsborough.

"Oh, yes, young Hilsborough," interjected Oldfield. "A bit of a harum-scarum and fond of the girls, but quite a good witness, I'd think. His news puts a different complexion on the case, doesn't it?"

"I'll say it does, Oldfield. I've just been thinking over matters on my way here in the 'bus. Do you know, it could very well have been Lorrimer who carried the unconscious Miss Tither to the cesspool and threw her in. Whether there was water there or not, he hoped to dispose of her, shall we say, by drowning or suffocation. Just for the sake of argument, shall we assume he spotted her being assaulted by Weekes and then, hurrying to the spot, found the farmer gone and the lady unconscious? He lifts her and carries her the short distance, pushes her in, closes the lid, and sneaks back home."

"Yes. That sounds reasonable enough. But why on earth should he run the risk of killing her, and with what motive?"

"There's something fishy about that Will, if you ask me, Oldfield. On the face of it, Lorrimer isn't concerned at all, but why should he take special care to try to turn Miss Tither against Wynyard? It wasn't as if he was going to benefit by the parson's being cut out. The whole went to charity. Which reminds me, I should be hearing something from the Yard in a day or so about the Home Alliance. But to get back to Lorrimer. He told me a deliberate lie when he said he was indoors, playing the piano most of the morning and particularly at the time we're interested in. Hilsborough saw him with Miss Tither. Now, suppose he sees from one of his upstairs windows—which, by the way, command a view of almost the whole village from the church to the manor house—suppose he sees Miss Tither crossing the fields in the direction of the Evingdon road. He knows from what she's already told him, that she's off to met Wynyard, so he keeps his eyes open and when he sees her returning, hares across the path which starts right opposite his gate, and runs through the manor park to the Evingdon road, just behind Haxley's house. He wants to know the result of the interview between Miss T. and Wynyard for some reason, and he wants to know it quickly. With a push, he must have encountered Miss Tither at the spot where Hilsborough saw them, near the stile. He gets to know what he wants and then returns the way he came."

Oldfield lit a cigarette and closely contemplated the glowing point.

"All the same, Littlejohn, that doesn't make him the murderer, does it? He's to get back unseen, look through the window again, and see Weekes assaulting the victim. Meanwhile, the maids have given him an alibi. He was playing the piano all the time. How do you get over that? Hilsborough *sees* him at one place; the maids *hear* him at another."

"That's just it, Oldfield. Remember, Hilsborough mentioned a player-piano? The instrument I saw at Lorrimer's house was a grand, and not a player. But the gadget Lorrimer bought was a separate fixture, removable at will, which converted an ordinary piano into a player. We must inspect that device to-morrow. Meanwhile, suppose it's electrical and can be left playing. That's another point, how long do the rolls of those things keep going?"

"I don't know, but I'll take you to someone to-morrow who'll soon tell us. Carry on."

"Well then, Lorrimer has made up his mind to get rid of Miss Tither if certain things have resulted from her interview with Wynyard, so he's on the look-out for her, on her return. He's got the piano playing to keep the servants thinking he's still at it in the drawing-room, and they know that while he's playing, he's not to be disturbed. When he spots Miss T., he dodges out by a quiet way, taking care not to be seen, and meets her on the highway. It's on the highway that his risk of being seen is greatest and if anyone spots him, he'll have to defer his plans to murder. There's nobody about, except a passing car—Hilsborough's—which is going so fast that it doesn't seem to matter. Miss T. tells Lorrimer something which signs her death-warrant. How or what Lorrimer planned to do is a puzzle, but whatever it was, he was prevented from doing it, because Weekes suddenly appeared in the field alongside. So Lorrimer sheered off home."

Oldfield puffed his cigarette thoughtfully.

"Seems sound enough, so far, although you'll admit it's mere conjecture. You might almost call it mere imaginary theorizin', mightn't you?"

Littlejohn grinned and agreed, filled and lit his pipe, and resumed.

"Yes, let's call it making the few facts we've got, square with a theory. Let's say, then, that Lorrimer sneaks back home. The piano's still at it; he puts on another record and goes to spy out what's happening in the direction of Tither. He sees Weekes in the act of striking the blow or else hurrying away, and what looks like a body on the ground in the vicar's field. He creeps off again, this time by a footpath behind the smithy and parallel with the road, which he crosses and enters the vicar's field. He finishes the job, crawls home once more. The piano's still playing. If no-one's seen him, he's got what he thinks is a good alibi with his servants. How's that?"

"Well, Littlejohn, in the parts of Yorkshire where I come from, they'd say it was very far-fetched. In other words, a great effort of imagination. All the same, it's a theory. Now it's up to us to test it. We'll set about it to-morrow morning. Don't forget Old Weekes's inquest is going to take some more of our time this week. Carradine, the Coroner, is in a rare temper about another inquest in Hilary Magna. He detests the place for some reason and seems to think the natives are doing it on purpose to spite him."

"There's another thing which interests me, Oldfield," continued Littlejohn. "Do you know anyone called Mossley, agent for some bank in the South Seas?"

"No. Why?"

"It seems he's the man who told Lorrimer about Wynyard's doings in the mission-field. He's manager at the town where Wynyard's stationed and is home on leave. Lorrimer met him in Evingdon the other week when Wynyard was lecturing there."

"I know nearly everybody, past and present, in this town and I've never heard of a Mossley. Besides, I told you I was at the lecture, didn't I? I didn't see any strange faces present, although Mossley might have been in the gathering. The room's small and the audience wasn't very large, though, and I can't see how I could miss seeing him."

"It looks to me as though Mossley is another imaginary figure in my scheme of things, then. Let's assume that Lorrimer got his story from Haxley, who has a pal in Pandalu, where Wynyard's stationed, and who writes and tells him all the horrid truth about this so-called labourer in the vineyard. Haxley told me the tale and said he'd mentioned it to Lorrimer. Perhaps Lorrimer invented a sort of Mrs. 'Arris for the purpose of making Miss Tither wise to Wynyard's bluff."

"He seems very anxious to do a dirty trick on Wynyard, doesn't he? Is it revenge, or gain?"

"That's to be found out, too."

"Quite a big programme for to-morrow."

"Yes. I think we'd better get Harriwinckle, or another of your men, on the job with me, if you can spare one."

"Yes. Suppose we let Harriwinckle enquire round the village concerning whether Lorrimer was seen stalking round about the time of the crime. I'll also send a man to Holly Bank when Lorrimer's out, to look into the player-piano business—make sure it's there. You and I will meet, get to know something about player-pianos from an expert, call to see Wynyard again and find out if he's had anything to do with Lorrimer in the past. We can try, too, those paths you suggested Lorrimer used while his piano was playing; to and from Miss Tither, conscious, and to and from Miss Tither, unconscious. That do?"

"Fine. And now I must be getting along. My dinner, or rather cold supper's waiting for me at 'The Bell'. Good-night."

"Good-night, Littlejohn. See you to-morrow, early. Sorry, I can't ask you home for a bite of something. We always have Sunday-evening meal with my mother-in-law at her house, and my wife's there waiting for me."

The following morning, the police carried on furtive activities in Hilary Magna. Harriwinckle, hot and important, slogged patiently round the place enquiring whom everyone had seen at or about the time of Miss Tither's death. Everybody seemed to have seen everybody else, including several people who saw Weekes passing through the village on his way to the vicar's field, but no one had seen his return. Jokes, rebuffs, impertinence, advice, free drinks, willing co-operation, P.C. Harriwinckle took them all with equanimity, but nowhere did he hear the name of Lorrimer mentioned. He reported disconsolately to his superiors, whom he had been trying to impress with his diligence. To his surprise, he received cordial thanks from Littlejohn and went home to his dinner in an elated frame of mind. "Well in with The Yard, oi be, mother," he said to his wife, as he sat down to a huge plateful of brisket of beef, potatoes, carrots, turnips and dumplings.

Meanwhile, Mr. Lorrimer having left his home immediately after breakfast on some unknown errand, a man who stated that he was the local A.R.P. inspector sent to examine garrets to ensure that all the inflammable lumber had been removed, arrived at Holly Bank and was allowed upstairs by the servants. He was so keen on his work, that he opened bedroom doors, too, greatly to the puzzlement of Alice, the kitchen-maid, who was sent to see that he did not run away with anything. In the box-room, the A.R.P. official took a strange interest in a small object, almost like a harmonium, which stood in one corner half hidden by trunks.

"That's a funny-lookin' thing, that is," said the visitor. "Better just look at it to see that it's not inflammable, or a petrol-driven engine or the like. Let's see. Whatever is it?"

"It's an orgin, I think. One of them things you plays on. Like a musical box. *You know*, a hurdy-gurdy," said Alice, who was thrilled by her job as guide to a handsome young man who smiled admiringly at her.

"Hurdy-gurdy. Well, I'll be blowed. Will it play?"

"Now don't you be doin' nothin' with that there. The master'll be woild if he even knows you bin in this room at all. Nobody's to meddle with his music. That's his instructions and he gets mad if he's not obeyed."

"How long's he had this thing... lemme see, wot's yer name?"

"Alice."

"Nice name for a nice gel. Well, Alice, how long's he 'ad this thing? Must be out o' date, eh?"

Alice's face glowed with pride.

"Oh, he's 'ad it about a year. I ain't never heard 'im play it. I never even seen it out of the room, except twice. But I did hear the master say he wanted it so's he could play duets by 'imself. Sounds mad to me."

"Queer folk some o' these toffs, ain't they, Alice?"

"I'll say they are. But you should 'ear the master on the pianner. Make it talk nearly, 'e can. Sometimes, when he's playin' the sort o' pieces they plays at the pictures like, you know, when the 'ero's tellin' his gel he loves 'er, sometimes when he plays like that, I cry me eyes out…"

A loud voice from below broke Alice's sentimental dream.

"Hey! Wot you two doin' up there so long?" shrieked Grace peevishly. "Thought you was inspectin' the garrets. It ain't proper you two hangin' about the bedrooms. Come you down at once, Alice, and let me 'ave no more of it."

The poor Alice fled below in confusion and P.C. Penrose, of the Evingdon force, hastily thanked the scowling Grace, bade her good morning, received no reply, and made his exit.

Littlejohn and Oldfield were, meantime, learning something about player-pianos from Major Crabtree, jack-of-all-trades of Evingdon. Mr. Crabtree's father, an ex-member of the Trentshire Yeomanry, had desired for his son a high army rank which his means were inadequate to procure. He therefore gave him Major as a Christian name, by which he had been known all his life, except during a spell as a conscript in the army, when he was ordered to assume the name of Wilfred by an outraged sergeant-major.

Crabtree received the two detectives in his shop, which was a mixture of antique-dealer's, marine-store, music emporium and second-hand bookseller's. Littlejohn wouldn't have been surprised if the owner had been a "fence" as well. "The Major" was without collar and coat, but he wore a black tie round his thick neck. His head was orange-shaped and covered with fine down. Teeth scattered and long, like diminutive piano-keys, yellow with age. Heavy paunch and thick arms and legs. He leered at his visitors. "Now, Inspector Oldfield, and what can I do for you this fine day, sir?" Major Crabtree did many things in the time at his disposal. He was a dealer, highly respected for his knowledge and shrewdness among the local fraternity. He was well read. He was a jeweller, too, and shy courting-couples, seeking a cheap engagement ring in private, invariably found blissful satisfaction in the room at the back of the junk-shop. He played the piano "by ear", and tuned most of the instruments in the town. He was also a good locksmith. On one occasion, he had opened the vault of a local bank after a clerk had lost the key, which feat caused the removal of the manager to a remote outpost and the replacement of the entire strongroom door by its outraged owners.

"Have you a player-piano in stock, Mr. Crabtree?" asked Oldfield, "because if you have, we'd like you to explain the mechanism and how long it takes to play a—a—record, do you call 'em?"

"Well, strike me! What'll you perlice be wantin' next? First of all, though, if I give advice, it'll be as an expert witness. Fee: five bob."

"Come, come, Major. No time for haggling. Let's get to business."

"Yes. I've got a player in the back room. Step along."

The dealer led the way through a maze of old furniture and odds and ends of all kinds, most of them reeking of decay and neglect, to a room even more cluttered with junk than the shop. In one corner stood an upright piano. The broker cleared a passage for himself and his visitors, who scrambled their way to the instrument.

"Not wantin' to buy one, are you, Inspector? I'll sell you this one cheap. Twenty pounds… complete with fifty rolls of the choicest music."

"No… I'm not interested in that aspect…"

"Fifteen quid then, take it or leave it…"

"*Will you shut up* and let me talk, Major."

The orange-headed man leered and chuckled, and lapsed into a teeth-sucking silence.

"Now I want to know what is the maximum length of time that one of these things will play, without changing the record or roll or whatever you call it."

"Well, that depends, Inspector. Rolls vary, o' course. Ten minutes, half an hour, three-quarters, even. Let's find the biggest o' the ones I got in stock, and we'll have a go, eh?"

The detectives had no wish to sit through a piano recital in the frowsy room, but this seemed to be the only way of checking their theory. Major Crabtree was fitting a roll in the contraption in anticipation.

"Very good then, Major. Get on with it, will you?"

The junk dealer drew up a battered music-stool and seated himself, portentously and with snortings, before the piano. He pushed back the frayed cuffs of his shirt, pulled up his shapeless trousers and sought the pedals with his feet.

"This is the longest piece I've got. *Jetty di Yew*, it's called. A good 'un. One of my favourites. Here goes."

Littlejohn glanced at the label of the empty case. *Jet d'Eau*. Proudly Major Crabtree trod out his masterpiece, an air with innumerable variations, apparently representing every kind of waterjet from fountains and geysers to garden hose and waste-pipes. On and on went the tinkling tune, sparkling cascades of sound, rippling, rumbling, rushing and roaring, with Mr. Crabtree quite immersed and oblivious of the group of small boys anxious to buy his foreign stamps, or the two women eager to dispose of household utensils. The Inspectors, having timed the start, waited anxiously for the end. It came at length, with the roll leaving the instrument with a crack and a whizz. Mr. Crabtree relaxed, reversed the gears and pedalled the broad strip of punched paper back on to the roll whence it had unwound. "Luvely!" he said, "Luvely! Twelve quid the lot. Bargain! Your last chance. Go on, ten quid. I'm losing money!"

"Oh, for heaven's sake, Major, dry up," said Oldfield, laughing. "That's taken nearly half an hour. Is that the average?"

"As I wuz sayin', Inspector, you can get 'em longer than that. Long Sonaters, List's Hungarian Rapsodaisicals, Chopine's Polonies, and sich like. Just depends on the piece. But when you're entertainin' company, barrin' dance tunes, who wants to sit for longer than half an hour listenin' to one piece on a pianner? Now, I ask you!"

"Well, we're both very much obliged for your help, Major, and remember, I owe you a good turn after this."

"Oh, don't mention it, Inspector Oldfield. Allis ready to 'elp the force. You know that."

On the way out, Littlejohn picked up a copy of *Twenty Five Years of Detective Life*, by his old favourite, Jerome Caminada, once of the Manchester police. He gave the Major a shilling for it and took it off in triumph for his friend Cromwell, of Scotland Yard.

Back at the police station quite a wealth of reports and information awaited them.

Harriwinckle had telephoned to say that he had searched fruitlessly round the village for anyone who had seen Lorrimer abroad at the time of the crime. He had also tried an experiment, suggested by his superiors over the telephone, and had successfully sneaked from Holly Bank to the stile on the Evingdon road and back, without being seen—or so he thought. Then, he had crept along the by-path behind the smithy to the scene of the crime, also unobserved—so he also thought.

P.C. Penrose had returned, changed back into uniform, and reported that he had found a player-piano in Holly Bank.

"That settles it," said Littlejohn. "Our next port of call is Holly Bank, again. I'm afraid Mr. Lorrimer's going to have to answer some difficult questions. By the way, before I go, did you go further into the matter of the manager of the bank in Pandalu?"

The sergeant-in-charge then told them that, as instructed, he had, during their absence, rung up the London Office of the English and Australian South Sea Bank. They had never heard of a Mr. Mossley. "Furthermore, neither they nor any other bank have a branch in Pandalu. There's a shipping and money-changing agency there, but no branch of any bank."

"The sooner we get to Holly Bank, the better. If Lorrimer can't give a satisfactory answer to our questions, we'd better arrest him. I think we've enough to support detention on suspicion. What do you say, Oldfield?"

"Yes. If you'll wait a minute, I'll swear out a warrant, just in case…"

Half an hour later, the two detectives entered the gravel drive of Mr. Lorrimer's villa and hurriedly rang the bell. Alice answered the door and Grace followed hard on her heels.

"Mr. Lorrimer in?" said Oldfield briskly.

Grace pushed her subordinate aside.

"No, he's not, sir. He went off about half an hour ago."

"Where did he go?"

"Can't say, sir. He came runnin' in all hot and flurried like. 'Has anybody called while h'I've been out?' sez he, and Alice tells 'im about the A.R.P. man and 'im so interested, like, in the organ thing upstairs. Almost 'it pore Alice, he did, in his temper. I've never seen 'im so mad and put about. Upstairs he goes and then down agen with his luggage. Two suitcases full. He went off in the car, then. 'I'll be away for a bit,' sez he, 'and if I'm not back by week-end, you two better take notice.' An' he gives us a five-pound note apiece, in spite of the fac' that Alice only gets half the wages I do. I never hear of nothin' like this. We're both packin' an' goin' to-day. We won't stop another day, not after the way 'e carried on…"

"All right, all right. Which way did he go?"

"Tuck the 'ilary Parver road… that leads to Evin'don; rahnda-bout, but quiet…"

Oldfield picked up the telephone and asked for Evingdon police station. Quickly he gave a description of Lorrimer and ordered an all-stations call to hold up the blue two-seater Benson coupé, described laboriously by the two maids. At length he hung up.

"Well, Littlejohn. Looks as if you were right, after all."

"Yes, the fox has gone to ground, Oldfield. Now we've got to dig him out."

CHAPTER XV

Commotion at Upper Hilary Farm

P.C. HARRIWINCKLE, HOT AND DESPONDENT, DRAGGED HIS heavy, perspiring feet along the Evingdon road in the direction of home. He had always regarded himself as the custodian of the villagers of Hilary Magna and the thought that one of them should escape his vigilance and hide himself successfully at the time when he was wanted by the law, was gall to him. Mr. Lorrimer seemed to have vanished from the face of the earth in a very short time and all the efforts of the police had not brought to light the slightest clue as to his whereabouts. Since his flight had been discovered, most of the county constabulary had been hunting the elusive little musician. Busmen, pedestrians, road-scouts, people in houses along the roads had all been questioned concerning the Benson coupé, but nobody had seen it.

"The thing couldn't a' took wings and flown," said P.C. Harriwinckle disgustedly to himself. On the way back to his station, he still persisted in his roadside enquiries without success. The stationmaster at Evingdon had been almost insulting.

"I war on duty frum nine, hay hem, until the last train at eleven, and if anybody boorded a train I'd a seen 'em. No use yew labourin' the point, Sam 'Arriwinckle. You'll not get me to admit as I might a' missed an odd one or two. This is a closed station, see, and nobody gets on it without showin' a tickut… I tells 'ee, Master Lorrimer caught no train yesterday or noight from 'ere.

An' now yew stop botherin' me. Wot I've said, I've said, see, and 'taint no use yew a-tryin' to catch me…"

Poor Sam's sergeant's stripes, which had dangled in his imagination since his prophetic dream, seemed to recede into the uncertain distance. During the past few days, when alone on his beat, the constable had amused himself by conducting imaginary conversations, in which he was addressed by a number of people as Sergeant Harriwinckle… Sadly he regarded a field pond in which cattle were standing knee-deep.

"Fer two pins, *Constable* 'Arriwinckle, I'd make an 'ole in that there water," he muttered, his morale broken by his lost hope and by his feet, which felt like two of his wife's suet-puddings, hot, heavy and sloppy. He halted at the by-road which led from the main thoroughfare up to Upper Hilary Farm. The highway was quiet; not a soul was in sight. Sheepishly the bobby looked to right and to left, furtively opened the gate, nipped through it and, squatting behind the tall, dust-covered hedge which divided the first field of the farm from the road, removed his boots and socks, took from his tunic pocket a fag-end, lighted it at the great risk of setting his moustache on fire, and relaxed. The grass was cool to his feet, the balmy air cleared his unhelmeted head and the tobacco gently stimulated him.

"Ahhhhhh…" said P.C. Harriwinckle and gently chid himself for being despondent. "Worse things nor that at sea," he said in an undertone and, with that philosophic consolation, he gave himself up to contemplating the scene.

The ground sloped gently away from the constable's pitch and he had a good view of the small farm and its buildings, which rested snugly in a small amphitheatre, for beyond the house, the land gently rose again. The homestead was of weathered, red, local brick, with a lichen covered, tile roof and gaunt chimneys. The house and dairy formed one side of a square; the barn, shippons, stables and coach-house making up the other three. The back door opened into a farmyard; the front, on the side remote from the constable, overlooked a small garden surrounded by tall trees and hazel bushes. The whole place might have been constructed to withstand a siege, so compact and enclosed did it seem.

The watching officer took it all in dreamily. He even noticed that the blinds of the house had not been drawn, although the late owner was lying in the mortuary. Mrs. Weekes had taken things strangely. She had not entered into mourning with the zeal expected of her by the village. Sure enough, everybody knew that the pair did not hit it off during the farmer's lifetime, but that was no reason for not assuming at least a semblance of grief at his decease in such a violent fashion. Mrs. Weekes seemed to bear her late husband a grudge for his hasty departure. He was to be buried from the morgue, even, and not to return to his farm. Furthermore, she had carried-on with the farm work as if nothing had occurred. Even as he meditated on her strange behaviour, Harriwinckle saw Mrs. Weekes emerge from the house and empty a bucket of garbage on the manure-heap in the middle of the farmyard. As she returned to the kitchen and closed the door, the constable's roving eyes turned to the tall chimneys. Several of them were smoking, white columns of wood-smoke rising straight into the still air. Sam Harriwinckle knew the farm well. In his mind's eye, he pictured the fires beneath the chimneys. The old brewhouse fire was hard at it; probably they were boiling water for calf meal on it, as they did in better days when he frequently called there. The kitchen, too. Cooking the dinner. The eccentric woman was going to have a hot meal, although alone and bereaved! Smoke was rising from the living-room fireplace, as well. Harriwinckle imagined the table laid for one and, as he dwelt upon the thought, he grew hungry himself. His hand strayed in the direction of his boots and then paused in mid-air. One of the bedroom chimneys was smoking, too!

"That's damned funny... she must have gone dotty. Never bin usedter 'avin' fires in their bedrooms... too greedy fer that... now what the hangment can that be for...?"

The constable assured himself that there was not another puff left in the quarter-inch of cigarette which remained and he thoughtfully ground it into the earth at his side. He meditatively drew on his boots and laboriously laced them. He put on his helmet, rose and straightened his tunic. His thoughts were elsewhere than on what he was doing, however. His sergeant's stripes loomed large again. His slow mind was working like a piece of heavy machinery. A thought seemed to strike him. He pondered it, his head on one side. Then, he apparently came to a decision and grew excited. Stirring himself into vigorous action, he picked up his rejuvenated feet and strode off in the direction of the farmhouse. As he entered the gate of the farmyard, the face of Mrs. Weekes appeared round the curtain of the kitchen window. She looked wild and scared. Her expression encouraged the constable in his business. He pulled up his belt, instinctively groped to see that the strap of his truncheon was handy and then knocked on the door. Better lift the latch, just in case... As he pressed his finger on it, he heard the woman fumbling with the bar, as though to fasten him out. Harriwinckle threw his weight against the door and thrust it ajar.

"Get away—get away! Can't you leave me alone? What have I done to be pestered?" moaned the woman, struggling to close the door again. Then, realizing that her efforts were vain, she suddenly relaxed. Harriwinckle, taken off his guard, plunged through the doorway and almost measured his length in the passage. Before he could recover himself, he was looking into the twin barrels of a sporting gun.

"Now get out, Sam Harriwinckle, and get going…"

"Now, now, Mrs. Weekes, don't you be a-goin' on so. I jest called to ask if there wuz anythin' you'd need helpin' on in the matter o' the inquest or other formalities, like. Put that there gun down, now. I knows you be overwrought a bit, but that's no excuse fer treatin' a h'officer that way. Put it down, and no more'll be said about the incidenk."

The woman looked wildly about. The policeman didn't like the look of her at all, nor of the gun she was holding. Her eyes were burning and her dishevelled hair, usually trim and neat, gave her a half-crazy appearance. Maybe she *had* gone crazy. Beads of sweat broke out under the policeman's helmet, seeped through and began to run down to his eyes. He removed his headgear and mopped his brow with a red handkerchief. Then, suddenly taking the helmet by the strap, he swung it hard against the barrels of the gun, momentarily deflecting them from his solar plexus. With his free hand, still clutching the handkerchief, he seized Mrs. Weekes's arm. She tussled to regain control of the gun and her fingers strained to raise the hammers, which, to Harriwinckle's comfort, he had noticed were not cocked. The woman seemed to have the strength of a maniac. Finally, she lost all restraint, clawed, beat, kicked and writhed against her assailant, breathing stertorously. For a minute, the pair struggled grimly.

"Mrs. Weekes, Mrs. Weekes, fer the love o' heaven 'ave some sense! Wotever are you a-thinkin' of...?" snorted the policeman with his remaining breath.

"Let me go... LET ME GO... or by the living God, I'll fill you full of shots like I did Weekes..."

In his horrified surprise, Sam Harriwinckle almost relaxed his hold and the full implication of what had been said dawning on him, he made a supreme effort and tugged desperately to disarm the demented woman. His foot slipped on the tiled passage, he involuntarily released his hold, and before he could recover, Mrs. Weekes had torn herself and the gun free. She stepped back a pace; the hammers clicked as she cocked them. Harriwinckle, in a flash, thought of his wife and his large family, of the police station, of the peaceful village which seemed so remote from him now. The explosion he was expecting to cut him short did not occur. Instead, the huge bulk of Inspector Littlejohn leapt from the gloom, two great arms encircled Mrs. Weekes, there was a blinding flash, a double report, and the rattle of shots in the ceiling. Harriwinckle was on his feet again, trembling...

Littlejohn was having his work cut out in mastering the woman. She was now quite out of control and fought like a demon. The village constable fished in his pockets, slung out a pair of handcuffs and, with surprising dexterity, snapped them on the wrists which encircled Littlejohn's neck. The Inspector slid his head from between the clinging arms and forced the woman back. Between them, they managed to get Mrs. Weekes to a chair and there they tied her with a rope, which Littlejohn cut down from the roof. She gnashed her teeth, blasphemed, uttered the most frightful oaths. Harriwinckle blushed at the sound of some of them. More footsteps. Inspector Oldfield entered and with him, held by a firm grip, was Lorrimer!

Harriwinckle's jaw fell. "So he wuz 'ere arter all?"

"Yes, Harriwinckle," answered Oldfield. "We had business here, too, and as we entered by the gate from the road, we saw you opening the kitchen door. Lucky for you we came, and lucky for us, too, because the noise you were making at the back, scared the fox out at the front and I managed to catch him by chasing him across the field. You've done a good morning's work, Harriwinckle."

Lorrimer, who had recovered his breath, was a sorry spectacle. He was unshaven, his linen was dirty, he looked as though he had not slept. His eyes were bloodshot and wild; his lips were dry and moved nervously, his hands opened and closed spasmodically.

"I can explain everything... I can explain everything... I protest against this treatment. I might be a criminal... Let go my arm... By God, I'll make you all sit up for this..."

"That will do, Mr. Lorrimer. You'll have an opportunity of explaining in due course. Meanwhile, I must caution you that anything you say may be used in evidence later. Now let's be moving."

The woman in the chair screamed wildly and gnashed her teeth. Then she burst into demoniacal laughter.

"Untie her, untie her... what are you doing to her...?" Lorrimer seemed suddenly to forget his own plight and discovered the condition of his companion in distress.

"Oh Annie, Annie, what have they done to you…? Untie her I tell you… What are you doing to her?" He was sobbing.

Oldfield turned to Harriwinckle. "You'd better harness up the dog-cart, I think, and I'll be getting back to the station with Mr. Lorrimer. We've some urgent questions to ask him. Perhaps you'll come with me, Littlejohn, and keep an eye on him while I drive. Harriwinckle can stay here until we can get a doctor and the asylum ambulance for Mrs. Weekes."

The constable cast a scared look at the woman, now quiet and mumbling, her lips flecked with foam.

"Perhaps Harriwinckle's had enough for one morning. He can drive you and I'll stay and wait for the ambulance," said Littlejohn.

The look he got from the harassed constable was ample reward for his thoughtfulness.

So, with drooping shoulders, a broken man, Lorrimer went to Evingdon between two police officers in a dog-cart, whilst Littlejohn, his pipe going, stayed to guard a mad woman, who did not speak a word or make another move until the ambulance arrived to take her to the Trentshire County Asylum.

CHAPTER XVI

Third from Left, Front Row

ON THE WAY TO EVINGDON POLICE STATION, LORRIMER SAT between the two policemen without uttering a word. He was haggard and drawn, his lips were an unhealthy red, his complexion chalky white, and his features strongly reminded Oldfield of a seasick traveller. The Inspector was so alarmed at his appearance that when they arrived at their destination, he gave him a seat in his office and offered him a drink of brandy, which Lorrimer eagerly accepted.

"And now, Mr. Lorrimer, perhaps you'd like to gather your thoughts together for a little while, preparatory to giving a statement of your recent movements and how you come to be involved in matters at Upper Hilary Farm. Just compose yourself until the Chief Constable and Inspector Littlejohn arrive," said Oldfield and he left his captive to cudgel his brains under the calm eye of Constable Harriwinckle.

A quarter of an hour later, Sir Francis Winstanley put in an appearance and was closeted with his Inspector for some time, until Littlejohn finally arrived. Then the three men joined Lorrimer and his custodian.

"How do you do, Lorrimer," said the Chief Constable blandly. "Been having an excitin' time, I hear. Now, we're willing to hear your account of things and I take it you've already been cautioned that whatever you say will be taken down in writing and may be used in evidence." Whereat, he summoned a young constable with a flair for shorthand writing, and settled himself comfortably to listen. Littlejohn looked at his watch. Harriwinckle fixed his eyes on the waiting shorthand expert and kept them wonderingly on him and his flying fingers for the rest of the session. The Hilary bobby made up his mind then and there, that all his offspring should learn this marvellous art as soon as he could arrange for them to do so.

"I protest against all this officious show," squeaked Lorrimer, who had somewhat recovered his composure and dignity. "Because I happen to be visiting Mrs. Weekes on an errand of condolence, it doesn't mean that I'm to be hauled here and accused of crimes you can't pin on anyone else. I demand to see my lawyer at once."

"Now, now, Mr. Lorrimer," interposed Oldfield, the self-appointed chairman of the gathering. "You're only making things more difficult for yourself. A reasonable statement from you may clear-up all your troubles. Why were you sneaking away from the Weekes's place? Why did you break into a run when you saw me approaching? And where were you last night?"

The last question brought a smile to Littlejohn's face. It reminded him of an old music-hall song. Lorrimer seized on it as a means of evading the two previous and more embarrassing queries.

"I stayed in Evingdon last night."

"Where?"

"The Saracen's Head."

"Did you garage your car there?"

"Yes… I mean, no. I put it in a garage for oiling."

"Wilkes at the garage didn't tell my man that when he

discovered your coupé there this morning. He said you left it, until called for, at ordinary garage terms."

"He may have misunderstood me."

"Why didn't you use your car for your trip to the farm?"

"I tell you it was under repair. Damn you, what are you driving at?"

"I'm suggesting that you stayed at Upper Hilary Farm last night in an effort to avoid our enquiries, Mr. Lorrimer."

"Nonsense."

"Very well. Will you kindly explain your movements on the morning of Miss Tither's death? In your original statement, you informed us that you were playing the piano the whole morning. Now we have evidence that you met Miss Tither on the Evingdon road shortly before her death. I suggest that you created an alibi for yourself by using a player-piano to deceive your servants into putting us off the track. Why did you do this?"

Lorrimer looked here and there as though seeking a means of relief or escape. He slumped despairingly in his chair.

"Very well. I'd better tell you what happened." He passed the tip of his tongue across his dry lips. His intent audience waited.

"I've been friendly with the Weekes for years. It's no news to you that Weekes himself has, for a long time, been a hopeless dipsomaniac. He's gone from bad to worse. Naturally, I did what I could, but he was too far gone when I found out what was happening. I, therefore, turned to lighten, as far as I could, the burden that brave little woman, his wife, was bearing. She was a deeply religious, kindly woman, totally unsuited for him. The strain has been too much for her... you saw what happened today... She's gone down under it."

Lorrimer paused, uttered a noise like a sob, and tears began to run down his cheeks.

Harriwinckle gaped. Surely, the man wasn't in love with that shrivelled, ill-tempered woman from Upper Hilary!

A pause, during which Lorrimer gathered up his wits and composed himself.

"The night before Miss Tither's death, Mrs. Weekes called on me after dark. Miss Tither had been to the farm, she said, and accused her husband of having an affair with Polly Druce, a well-known bad lot, and Weekes had threatened to kill her for what she'd told his wife. I pacified her and told her his threats, made under liquor, would never materialize. The following day, however, I thought it best to warn Miss Tither to be careful what she said and what she did when Weekes was about. I was playing over a roll on my player-piano attachment, when I saw her in the distance on the Evingdon road. What better time to tell her? Leaving the instrument playing in my haste to catch her, I went through the french window, crossed the field, and hailed her. When I'd warned her, I returned. Judge of my horror and surprise, when I saw Weekes, who didn't see me, by the way, crossing the field-path in the direction of the gap in the vicarage hedge. I'd met Miss Tither on the road, however, so, thinking their paths wouldn't cross, I returned home. The next thing I heard was that Miss Tither had been found dead in the vicar's cesspool... What was I to do? Volunteer information to the police and bring further distress on the Weekes—or rather on Mrs. Weekes? Or keep it dark? I decided on the latter course. Weekes couldn't live long at any rate. I wanted to keep the stigma of being a murderer's wife from Mrs. Weekes, if I could. She's suffered enough already.

Provided some other was not falsely accused, I could see no harm in silence... I faked a tale to the police to put them off the track of Weekes. That's all I have to say."

Harriwinckle tore his eyes from their wondering stare in the direction of the shorthand writer, and looked at his superiors. The Chief Constable was yawning; Littlejohn, his legs stretched out straight in front of him, was regarding the tips of his brightly polished shoes meditatively; Oldfield looked red, angry and ready to explode at any moment. Lorrimer gazed from one to the other with a mixture of cunning and effrontery. Was there, in his manner, something of that of a schoolboy, awaiting the results of an examination before his teacher, or of the effects of his school report on his father? P.C. Harriwinckle thought of his own son, Harry...

Just then, a car drew up outside the police station and footsteps sounded in the corridor. The head of Detective-Sergeant Cromwell, of Scotland Yard, was thrust in, his eyes sought the big form of his chief and lit up. Littlejohn smiled and nodded a greeting. "Ah, Cromwell! At last," he said and introduced his colleague to the rest of his companions. Cromwell held a whispered conversation with his chief and retired. The sound of footsteps again and then there entered Miss Livermore, of Chitty, Mulliner and Passey, London. Her eyes fell on Lorrimer at once.

"Well, Mr. Jenkinson!" she almost screamed. "Who'd have thought of meeting you here?"

The effect on Lorrimer was electric. He leapt to his feet like one stung.

"Blast you, what are you doing here...?" he yelled.

"Really, Mr. Jenkinson… I never did… really. All I was asked to do by the police was to call here to identify a client… Why, Mr. Jenkinson, you must have been called here for the same purpose. What a waste of time…"

"Get out… get out. You've done damage enough, damn you."

Miss Livermore, bewildered, was assisted into the next room by Cromwell, who seemed to leave her in safe hands and then returned to the main gathering.

Oldfield rose.

"Crispin Lorrimer, alias Theodore Jenkinson, I arrest you for the murder of Ethel Tither, and I warn you that anything you say will be taken down in writing and may be used in evidence."

"What, again!" bleated Lorrimer. "I never heard such tomfoolery in my life. Jenkinson! Murderer of Tither! What's the meaning of all this nonsense?"

Littlejohn rose patiently to his feet and placed an old, faded photograph before Lorrimer.

"Do you recognize the third figure from the left, front row, on that? You've changed a bit, Mr. Lorrimer, since the days when you had that taken at Hunstanton on Titmuss's annual outing. My colleague here secured that print from Mr. Titmuss himself. He also learned that you were then known as Jenkinson, your true name, I believe. You are proprietor of the firm of Chitty, Mulliner and Passey, of London, the accountants of the charity to which Miss Tither was leaving quite a considerable legacy. Not only are you accountant to the Home Alliance, you are founder, faker and general manager of it. In fact, you *are* the Home Alliance. Your general factotum, Mortimore, was arrested this morning on suspicion of being a confidence trickster, and made a full confession…"

Livid with fury, Lorrimer flung himself on Littlejohn in an attempt to escape to the door. The Inspector pushed him back in his chair with little effort.

"Now, Mr. Lorrimer, or Jenkinson, do you wish to modify your statement, bearing in mind that we also know that, according to the church register here, Weekes married one Annie Jenkinson, your sister?"

Lorrimer gazed stupidly up at Littlejohn. His eyes grew glassy. He fought for breath.

"She was dead when I found her. I tell you she was dead. I threw her in the cesspool to hide her. I wanted to save my sister from disgrace… my sister Annie…"

Then he fell on the floor in a dead faint.

CHAPTER XVII

Thornbush Comes Clean

THE ARREST OF MR. LORRIMER FOR THE MURDER OF MISS Tither created a sensation which shook the Hilarys to the roots. Knots of natives discussed it for days and occupied a lot of time in comparing notes concerning their business and encounters with that viper which the community had so long nursed in its bosom, the occupant of Holly Bank. It was during this long spate of tittle-tattle, that P.C. Harriwinckle forged the last link in the chain of evidence against Lorrimer, alias Jenkinson.

The village constable knew that Littlejohn was anxious concerning the fact that nobody had seen Lorrimer anywhere near the scene of the crime after Weekes had committed the first part of it. True, the accused had betrayed himself at the police station in front of witnesses, and then fainted. But the case would be all the more invulnerable if defending counsel were unable to cast doubt on the man's whereabouts. It would be more watertight and ship-shape if someone had seen Lorrimer going to or from the cesspool or its locality. Harriwinckle spent tireless days and sleepless nights endeavouring to find the last piece of the puzzle, which, he was sure, would bring with it the precious three stripes.

One day, as he was eating his suet dumplings for lunch, the constable confessed to his wife that he "was beat".

"I've searched 'igh and low, mother, in the 'opes of bringing me quoter of evidenks and findin' somebody as was near the scene of the crime and see the h'accused in proximincty, but I gives it up. Nobody seen 'im. It's wormwood and gall to me, mother. An' this my biggest case and real chanct to make a job of it."

Mrs. Harriwinckle swallowed hard, the better to make sympathetic clucking with her mouth.

"Don't go on so, Sam. You'll give yourself indig-gestion and all to no good purpose. Wot 'as to be, 'as to be, and nothin' we can do can make it otherwise, I allus says. Here's you, itchin' to be comin' forward with evidenks that'll 'ang a man; and there's old Walter Thornbush, a-offering up prayers 'cos his hasn't been needed."

P.C. Harriwinckle paused, his mouth open, an impaled dumpling half-way *en route*. His eyes bulged.

"Wot's that you sez, mother?" he asked with eager menace.

"Mrs. Wellings,—one of the Emmanuel's Witnesses, she be—wuz a-tellin' of me this mornin' that Thornbush mentioned it in 'is prayer at the meetin' last night."

The constable flung down his knife and fork, picked up his helmet and, fastening his belt on the way, rushed into the village street.

"Hey, Sam, Sam! Wot about the treacle-puddin'?" howled his wife after him, but her husband was out of earshot.

Walter Thornbush was eating his dinner of sandwiches on an overturned box in his wheelwright's shop when Harriwinckle hastily entered.

There was fine dust in Walter's hair and sawdust all over his clothes. He looked to have been rolling in the by-products of his craft.

"Look 'ere, Thornbush," said Harriwinckle, without preamble. "Wot's all this about you a-offering public prayers on account o' bein' spared from givin' evidenks? Now, wot is this evidenks? I demands to know."

Thornbush chewed meditatively, cleared his throat and looked the constable impudently in the face.

"The accused having been arrested, it h'isn't your business to be cross-h'examining me, Sam Harriwinckle. By divine dispensation, I've been spared the 'orror of testifying against my fellow man. For that I proffered 'umble thanks to Gawd at the meetin' last night. And rightly so, too. Vengeance is mine, saith the Lord, I will repay."

"That's enough o' that, Walter Thornbush. No more texes, if you please. Facts is wot I wants, and facts I'm gon' to 'ave. Now, wot evidenks have you been withholdin' from the law, and why, when I called 'ere to see you, didn't you disclose same to me as you oughter?"

"Because, I wasn't goin' to be having the blood of a fellow man on my 'ands. My principles forbids it, Sam 'arriwinckle."

"Unless you tells me wot it is at once, I shall treat you as an excessary arter the fact; as withholding wital information from the police and h'obstructin' same in the execution of their duties; and I shall see that you're sub-peenied to give testimony under h'oath in the court and at the same time be treated as an 'ostile witness."

Beneath such a load of legality and guilt, Thornbush quailed. He almost fell backwards from his perch and took quite a time to recover his poise and speech.

"Hostile witness?" he said. "No Emmanuel's Witness can be hostile."

"Oh yes they can, and the law makes it 'ot for them."

"Oh, well, if it comes to that, I may as well tell you. The man's been arrested at h'enny rate. My bit won't make any difference. I saw him crossing the field behind the smithy about the time o' Miss Tither's death. Saw 'im come back, too. He was sneakin' along, like, and thought I didn't see him. I was in the darkness of my shop and could see without bein' seen."

Beside himself with excitement, Sam Harriwinckle took down times, dates and a statement from the wheelwright, and went on his way home rejoicing. He telephoned his news to the Evingdon police and then, having jauntily hung up the receiver, sought out his wife, who was washing-up in the kitchen and grumbling loudly to herself at her husband's lack of consideration for the culinary treats which she was at pains to prepare for him in the shape of treacle-puddings and the like. Seizing her round her ample waist, P.C. Harriwinckle planted a noisy, rousing kiss on her mouth.

"Ma, blest if yew ain't a better detective nor the lot of us! Yew've given me the crucicle clue of the case," he said.

Mrs. Harriwinckle, hot and confused, blushed modestly and almost buried her face in the dishcloth in her confusion.

"Go on with you, Sam," she said. "Wot things you do say."

Later, at a conference held in the library of Sir Francis Winstanley's home, Littlejohn was asked by the Chief Constable to give Oldfield and himself a running account of his reconstruction of the crime. As Sir Francis remarked, the Scotland Yard man's report would be the Crown's case in Rex v. Jenkinson and, before a formal statement was submitted to the Public Prosecutor, they might as well turn over the details in free-and-easy fashion and make themselves familiar with them.

With his pipe glowing and a glass of whisky at his elbow, Littlejohn began his story.

"The death of Miss Tither is really the end of Jenkinson's, or Lorrimer's, life of crime. Let's call him Lorrimer, it seems to fit better. He was a brainy lad and ambitious, but seems to have held himself in check until his head got turned by associating with those outside his class and income in the last war. Then, when he was demobilized, he started his confidence-trickster's game. From Mortimore, since his arrest, and from the documents impounded at the Home Alliance office, we get a pretty picture of his doings. For the past ten years, he's carried on this bogus charities racket. As the Rev. Dr. Scarisdale—elusive and non-existent—he posed as a reformer, but never allowed himself to be seen. With the help of Mortimore, he discovered charitable-minded people, mostly elderly and unbusinesslike ladies, with gullible dispositions, and pestered them for contributions to his work, which, as the means of rescuing fallen women, seems specially to appeal to that class of subscribers. They made five thousand a year out of it in sums— many of them substantial—from all over the country. If anyone got curious, there was always Jenkinson—again Lorrimer—with his firm of warranted accountants, of long standing and repute— to sign the balance-sheet and add tone to the accounts."

"A very pretty idea," interposed Sir Francis, "but rather risky. Suppose someone had insisted on seein' Scarisdale or actual fruits of the labours of the Home Alliance? And suppose it had come out that there was 'no sich person' or fruits?"

"Well, I suppose, sir, that the type of subscriber to such chari-ties, isn't very curious that way. Provided they get accounts, flat-tering letters, and plenty of literature on the subject, they don't ask questions. That's why Miss Tither came to grief. She was a busybody, who wouldn't be put off, and put Lorrimer's little game in danger by threatening—not vindictively, but from curiosity—to have it investigated."

Littlejohn drank up his whisky and continued.

"From what I can gather, Lorrimer took up his residence here to be near his sister, Mrs. Weekes. They were natives of Hilary, remember, but left the place when they were children. Annie, the girl, returned with her father, but Lorrimer stayed in rooms in Trentbridge and grew out of recognition by the natives. Then, having assured himself of an income from his confidence enterprises, he returned here. He and his sister were strangely attached and perhaps, hearing of her misalliance with Weekes and the turn events had taken, he bought Holly Bank to be near her. Probably Weekes himself didn't know that Lorrimer was his brother-in-law."

Sir Francis filled up Littlejohn's glass and the detective, after re-lighting his dead pipe, took up the tale.

"Lorrimer hadn't been in Hilary long, before he chose Miss Tither as a likely one to pluck for his Home Alliance. She was abnormally interested in the sexual wrong-doings of the village. That made her a good one to tackle for subscriptions for fallen women elsewhere. From headquarters in London, therefore, began a steady stream of importunate letters. Miss Tither was gulled into thinking she was supporting a great work, was made a vice-president, and opened her purse liberally. Not only that, she expressed an intention of leaving a legacy to the society. We may take it that Lorrimer soon got to know the extent of the legacy. That was good, but not enough for him. He wanted all he could get, so having discovered that Miss Tither's next-of-kin, Wynyard, was legatee, he set about discrediting him, by embellishing a tale which Haxley had told him and fobbing it off on Miss Tither with a show of innocent gossip. She fell for the plan and wrote giving Wynyard an opportunity of clearing himself."

"But what good was a legacy to Lorrimer?" interposed Oldfield. "If she didn't die first, he'd have had to kill her to get it. Rather a risky price to pay, eh?"

"Yes, but he was ready to take it. The impounded books and papers of the Home Alliance showed a huge falling-off in subscriptions, probably owing to the war. The type of people who give to such societies are usually elderly ladies and such like, with fixed incomes. The war's hit that class hard and charitable subscriptions are the first to feel the axe. Furthermore, Miss Tither wrote a letter, which we found in the files, to the effect that she proposed asking a friend of hers, a stockbroker in the City, to investigate the Home Alliance, in view of the fact that she proposed to leave an increased legacy to it in her Will. Such a step would have been fatal. A thoroughgoing business man, let loose among the Home Alliance accounts would have seen through the swindle right away. Lorrimer and Mortimore, the latter by a personal visit to Hilary, tried to put her off, and succeeded in doing so for a time, but she being of a ferreting, inquisitive nature, couldn't be quietened for long, and finally insisted. That signed her death-warrant.

"I don't know why Miss Tither was in such a pother about making what she called an emergency Will. We can assume, however, that in her conversation with Lorrimer on Sunday, he'd so played on her feelings, that she drew a document herself and executed it before Russell and Thornbush. Perhaps Lorrimer mentioned the risk of Wynyard's doing her violence on hearing that she proposed to alter her Will and cut him out. On the other hand, she may have mentioned the threatening attitude of the Weekes man and woman and Lorrimer again might have suggested she should make the Alliance legatee for the residue of her estate in what she called the emergency document. In any case, there was the new Will. That gave Lorrimer two motives; the shutting of Miss Tither's mouth lest the Home Alliance be investigated, and his need for money which the Will would give him, and, under the new document, in large quantities. He was so eager to know the result of her interview with Wynyard and, presumably, whether or not she'd taken his advice and drawn up a new Will, that he hastened to meet her on her way back from Satchell's café. The news he got from her then, sealed her fate. On the first opportunity, and there were many with a prowling woman of her kind, he would kill her. He left her and returned to Holly Bank. Then, looking from the window at home, he sees something which presents him with the very chance he'd been seeking. Weekes is quarrelling with Miss Tither and finally strikes her to the ground and sheers off. Lorrimer sneaks to the scene of the crime, hoping she's dead. Instead, he finds her still breathing and with a good chance of recovering consciousness. He is unarmed and wonders how to finish her off. He remembers the cesspool. Hastily, he carries the body there and opens the lid, only to find the place clean and dry. He turns on the tap from the first tank and a slow trickle of water begins to run in. He thrusts the body in the pit, face down, closes the trap and creeps away. If she doesn't drown, she'll suffocate."

"But what about Weekes?" said Sir Francis. "Surely, Lorrimer would quietly have tried to put the blame on him, if he could. It was known by Russell, for example, that Weekes had threatened Miss Tither. Furthermore, one would think that Lorrimer would have jumped at the chance of freeing his sister from the whisky-sodden husband's clutches."

"For some reason or other, he didn't, and I'm sure it was at the wish of his sister. Didn't she say, 'Vengeance is mine.' She was killing off Weekes in her own way with the whisky bottle. Had she taken a firm stand with him when first he started drinking, he would probably never have become a drunkard at all. But she despised him. He was beneath her and the longer she lived with him, the more she hated him. When, however, Weekes confessed to me that he had attacked Miss Tither, matters changed. Don't forget, Weekes had probably seen Lorrimer in the vicinity. He was coming with me to the police station and his wife didn't know what he'd say once he got there and under fire. To prevent his incriminating her brother, whose means of livelihood, whose double life, and whose association with Miss Tither she was aware of, for brother and sister were in the habit of secretly meeting at Holly Bank, she acted quickly, shooting her husband with the shotgun and making it appear as suicide. She was a cunning one, with a craft born of madness. Her mother died in an asylum and she took after her. Somehow, she must have guessed who committed the crime; perhaps she saw Lorrimer about the place on the morning of the murder. When her brother, hunted by the police, sought refuge at her farm and Harriwinckle, attracted by the smoking of a chimney which wasn't accustomed to doing so, suspected that someone was lying doggo there and went to enquire, she was quite prepared to use the gun on the policeman, too."

"What a queer, even grotesque crime it is," said Sir Francis. "Hearing of it, one seems to lose a sense of reality. The atmosphere of that strange farm, the couple living there, getting on each other's nerves, hating and ready to murder. And across the village, another man, nursing crime, wondering how his sister was faring, yet unable to come into the open on her side, lest he disclose his identity."

"Yes. How well he preserved it! Mortimore knew him as Jenkinson and knew that he was using his powers as an accountant to commit his swindling, but he didn't know where his hide-out was, or what name he assumed. All correspondence was accumulated at the office for him. Jenkinson arrived once a week from goodness knows where and, having given Mortimore his instructions and drawn his share of the spoils, vanished into the blue again. Luckily for us, Cromwell got the old photograph from Mr. Titmuss. It was taken long ago, but the features were there, the pointed nose, the queer shaped, almost hydrocephalic head, and that put us on the track. When Jenkinson and Lorrimer turned out to be one and the same, the fog cleared, didn't it?"

Sir Francis rose, indicating that the session was at an end. "Well," he said, "I think we've got a good case. Now it's up to Counsel for the Crown."

At his trial, Crispin Lorrimer, alias Theodore Jenkinson, was as cool as a cucumber in the dock. One would have thought, from his bearing, that he was a spectator at some kind of contest which was staged for his pleasure.

Mr. Claplady, showing signs of emotion at testifying against one who had once been a member of his flock, told of the cesspool, the strange life of the Weekes's, the occurrences in the village on the morning of the crime. Isaiah Gormley, dressed more picturesquely than ever, figured almost as an expert witness on cesspools and caused the prosecution a lot of trouble, patience and fruitless sarcasm before he ended his tale. Mr. Haxley, after refusing to take the oath, told Prettypenny's tale of Wynyard's life in Pandalu, which Wynyard shamefacedly confirmed, and the Crown brought out Lorrimer's embellishments and his creation of a fictitious bank-manager for his purpose. The accused, at this point, nodded approvingly as though admiring his own fertile imagination.

Miss Satchell, Hilsborough, Haxley and, finally, Walter Thornbush, who made great play with the oath, fixed the relative positions of Lorrimer and Miss Tither at the time of the crime and Littlejohn gave particulars concerning Weekes's confession and death. Mortimore, turned King's Evidence, Cromwell, and a sworn statement from Mr. Titmuss, who was unfit to travel, laid bare all the affairs of the Home Alliance, and Miss Livermore, red-nosed and affronted at being associated with a criminal firm, blew Chitty, Mulliner and Passey wide open to the winds of circumstance and indignantly repeated that Crispin Lorrimer and Theodore Jenkinson were one and the same person. The accused bowed to her from the dock. The relations between Lorrimer and Mrs. Weekes, now hopelessly insane and detained in the County Asylum, were firmly established by history and state records.

There was nothing between Jenkinson and hanging but the speech of his counsel. Mr. Morton Bagshawe, K.C., did his best. He laughed at the idea of a crime which nobody had witnessed. He scouted the player-piano alibi, in spite of the fact that two maids had sworn that their master went raving mad and ran away from home after discovering that the police had learned that such an instrument was in his possession. "Gentlemen," he said to the jury, "you're not going to let two hysterical servant-girls exaggerate a situation into a life-and-death matter, and in their search for notoriety, make a mountain out of a molehill."

The verdict was "guilty", however. It was only when the judge, wearing a strange strip of black stuff atop his wig, pronounced the fatal words, that the accused seemed to realize what was happening. It was then that Jenkinson, "the most cold-blooded and cowardly skunk I've ever taken on"—those were Bagshawe's words *sub rosa*—it was then that Jenkinson turned ashen, clutched the rails of the dock, howled blasphemies at the judge, and was finally borne away yelling and struggling by his guards. He was hanged after an unsuccessful appeal. When he finally realized that nothing could save him, Jenkinson wrote out a long and boastful confession which he addressed to Littlejohn. This statement bore out to a remarkable degree the story constructed by Littlejohn from the information and clues he and his colleagues had gathered. "I have my doubts as to whether or not he should be in Broadmoor," commented the prison chaplain as he handed Littlejohn the letter. After he had read it, the detective almost agreed.

CHAPTER XVIII

Repercussions

M RS. WEEKES NEVER RECOVERED HER SANITY AND IS STILL detained during His Majesty's pleasure.

Littlejohn, who made a trip to Evingdon to terminate certain formalities and took the 'bus to Hilary to stay the night with his friend, the landlord of "The Bell", found the little village quite recovered from the unhappy events of the autumn. It was an early spring day when he arrived, the air was unusually warm, and before he departed to catch his train, Littlejohn enjoyed a stroll round the place. The Rev. Athelstan Wynyard was in residence at Briar Cottage. He had established his rights to Miss Tither's estate after the exposure of the bogus charity and had forthwith resigned and rested from his labours in the South Seas. Sarah Russell had left the place to marry a farmer in the neighbouring village. Walter Thornbush, more vociferously religious than ever through his matrimonial disappointment, was toiling at his wheels as Littlejohn passed the door of his shop. Walter's hair and clothes were, as usual, covered in the off-scourings of his craft, and he looked as though he had recently plunged head-first in wood chippings and sawdust.

Calling at the vicarage to greet Mr. Claplady, Littlejohn was surprised to find him not at home and the living in charge of a young curate. The detective was cordially received.

"Mr. Claplady is in London at present at the Department of Apiculture, where he is abridging his unpublished work on Bees to the size of a thirty-page pamphlet in aid of the government's bee-keeping drive. The village regards it as a high honour and will welcome him back as a celebrity."

On the Evingdon road, just past Miss Satchell's busy tea-room, Littlejohn met a proud figure, strolling portentously on his round of guarding the village. It was Sergeant Samuel Harriwinckle, resplendent in a new tunic with three proud stripes on his sleeve. From his top pocket protruded the silver chain of a combination watch and guard, presented to their guardian by his fellow-villagers to mark his promotion. Littlejohn congratulated the worthy man heartily.

"H'offered me a position in the Evin'don force, they did," said Sam, blushing under Littlejohn's praise, "but, 'No,' oi sez. 'No. The willage where I won me stripes is good enough for me. In fac', I'd rather not have me stripes, if it's all the same to yew, than leave me willage.' At which they laughed and said I wuz too modest, but that it wuz all the same to them. So 'ere oi be, sir, and thanks to yew and wot yew done for me."

"Not at all, Harriwinckle. You contributed your share to the solution of the problem, just like all the rest of us. We were a good team and one couldn't have done without the others."

And each went on his way thinking the other a jolly good fellow.

Two months later two books arrived at Littlejohn's home. One was a technical journal and, following indications heavily marked in the index, the detective found an article on "Birds in a Suburban Garden", by Titmuss and Cromwell. Flabbergasted, he turned to the other packet. This was endorsed with the author's compliments and turned out to be *Bee Keeping for Victory*, by Ethelred Claplady, M.A. (Cantab.).

Laughing, the detective turned to his wife.

"It's a good job we live in a top-floor flat," he said. "These two johnnies would be roping me in with their bird and bee keeping, otherwise."

And he curiously opened another parcel, also addressed to him in Mr. Claplady's spidery hand. It contained practical evidence of that good man's activities—honey in the honeycomb.

Dear Reader,

We want to tell you about George Bellairs, the forgotten hero of British crime writing.

George Bellairs wrote over fifty novels in his spare time (his day job being a bank manager). They were published by the Thriller Book Club run by Christina Foyle, manager of the world famous Foyle's bookshop, and who became a friend. His books are set at a time when the real-life British Scotland Yard would send their most brilliant of sleuths out to the rest of the country to solve their most insolvable of murders. Bellairs' hero, gruff, pipe-smoking Inspector Littlejohn appears in all of them. Though his world might have moved on, what drove people to murder—jealousies, greed, fear—is what drives them now. George Bellairs' books are timeless.

If you liked this one, why don't you sign up to the George Bellairs mailing list? On signing you will receive exclusive material. From time to time we'll also send you exclusive information and news.

So join us in forming a George Bellairs community. I look forward to hearing from you.

www.georgebellairs.com
George Bellairs Literary Estate